Christmas is a time for giving

Gifts are not always things you can hold
in your hands. The gift we celebrate at
Christmas is that small baby born in a stable,
though the shepherds and the wise men did
manage to bring presents as well.

These books also celebrate Christmas, and
each deals with a different gift, the kind that
can bring immeasurable love and contentment
down the years—which we wish for all of you.

Enjoy!

Laura MacDonald lives in the Isle of Wight, and is married with a grown-up family. She has enjoyed writing fiction since she was a child, but for several years she worked for members of the medical profession, both in pharmacy and in general practice. Her daughter is a nurse and has helped with the research for Laura's medical stories.

Recent titles by the same author:

A SECOND CHANCE AT LOVE
HOLDING THE BABY

A KIND OF MAGIC

BY
LAURA MACDONALD

*First published in Great Britain 2000
Large Print edition 2001
Harlequin Mills & Boon Limited,
Eton House, 18-24 Paradise Road,
Richmond, Surrey TW9 1SR*

© Laura MacDonald 2000

ISBN 0 263 16842 5

*Set in Times Roman 16½ on 18 pt.
17-0601-51845*

*Printed and bound in Great Britain
by Antony Rowe Ltd, Chippenham, Wiltshire*

CHAPTER ONE

THE first time Staff Nurse Sophie Quentin set eyes on the new paediatric registrar he was on his knees, and at that point she didn't even know his name. It was in the brightly coloured play area of the children's ward with its large, plastic toys and Disney-style posters and he was kneeling beside a red table, helping a small boy to construct a precarious-looking tower with chunky pieces of Lego. Sophie had just come from Sister Bailey's office, where they had both been struggling with staff rotas, and was preparing to meet a new patient who would shortly be arriving on the ward with her family.

She paused for a moment beside the table, looking down on the two heads close together in concentration, the fair tousled head of the child and the dark, but equally tousled head of the man. 'That doesn't look very safe,' she commented, and both heads turned and two pairs of eyes looked up at her. The little boy's eyes were blue, extraordinarily blue, while the man's were a rich hazel flecked with green.

'Hello, Thophie,' the child lisped.

'Hello, Harry.' Sophie smiled back, aware that the man was staring at her with interest.

'Dr Lawrenthe ith helping me—we're trying to make the biggetht tower ever.' Harry's voice rose in excitement. 'We're going to uthe every thingle piethe of Lego, aren't we?' he demanded earnestly, turning and looking directly into the man's face.

'Well, we're going to have a jolly good try,' the man replied.

'I don't think we've met,' said Sophie.

'No,' he agreed, 'I don't believe we have.' Setting the last block on the top of the tower— accompanied by a whoop of delight from Harry—he struggled to his feet and held out his hand. 'Benedict Lawrence,' he said. 'Mr Crowley-Smith's registrar.'

'Pleased to meet you. Sophie Quentin.' She put her hand in his and was vaguely aware that he held it a fraction longer than was strictly necessary. 'Have you met Sister yet?'

'No.' He shook his head, at the same time finally releasing her hand. 'I was on my way to her office when I was waylaid by this young man who required my help with this construction job. In the end it was a question of priorities.'

'Oh, absolutely.' Sophie laughed and he joined in, the hazel eyes creasing at the corners, the lips parting to reveal strong, even, white teeth. On first acquaintance she liked him but, then, she would probably like anyone who put the needs of a child before anything else. It was one of the reasons she herself chose to work on Paediatrics.

'But now that the job is complete maybe it's time I moved on.' Reaching down, the registrar ruffled the boy's hair. 'Is Sister in her office?'

'Yes, she is.' Sophie nodded. 'I'll take you through.' Leaving Harry quietly demolishing the tower that had so painstakingly been constructed, Sophie led the way through the children's ward, retracing her steps to Sister's office. They met Hazel Bailey on her way out. A small bird-like figure, with sharp eyes behind gold-rimmed spectacles that missed nothing, her gaze flew from Sophie to the registrar, who stood there in his white coat with the buttons undone, his stethoscope protruding from his top pocket, then questioningly back to Sophie again.

'Sister, this is Dr Lawrence, our new registrar,' Sophie explained. 'I gather he was on his way to see you but he got waylaid.'

'I'd almost given you up, Dr Lawrence,' said Sister Bailey with the air of one who's not used to being kept waiting.

A sheepish look crossed Benedict's features and, to her amazement, Sophie found herself leaping to his defence. 'It was Harry who waylaid him,' she explained. 'A pressing matter of a Lego construction.'

'Ah, I see.' Sister Bailey nodded and an understanding expression replaced the frown that had been on her face. 'Well, Dr Lawrence, now that you're here, maybe you'd like to have a look around. We're expecting a visit from Mr Crowley-Smith later this morning so I'm sure you'd like to familiarise yourself with the place before then.' She paused. 'Sophie, would you like to show Dr Lawrence around?'

'Well, yes.' Sophie hesitated. 'Although I do have Chloe Stewart coming in shortly.'

Sister Bailey glanced at her watch. 'You have a quarter of an hour before Chloe arrives.

I have a meeting to attend. I'll see you later, Dr Lawrence.' With that she bustled away, leaving Sophie and Benedict standing outside her office.

'I bet you thought you had time for a quick coffee before your patient arrived,' said Benedict with a grin.

'Chance would be a fine thing.' Sophie pulled a face. 'Come on, we'd best get going otherwise there'll be no time to show you anything. Now, where would you like to start, Dr Lawrence?'

'How about down there in Teletubby land?' He nodded towards the far end of the ward, where a section of cots was surrounded by screens decorated with the brightly coloured characters from the popular television series.

'OK.' Sophie nodded. 'Dipsy and La-La, here we come.'

'And by the way,' he said as they made their way down the ward, 'the name is Benedict, or Ben if you prefer.'

When Sophie nodded again, he said, 'May I call you Sophie?'

'Please, do,' she replied. 'It's very informal on this ward—it helps to relax the children. They all use first names.'

'Even Sister Bailey's?' he asked, raising dark eyebrows.

'Ah, she's possibly the exception, and maybe your boss, Mr Crowley-Smith, is another… Although…' Sophie paused '…having said that, we did have one little girl once who asked him what his name was.'

'And did he tell her?'

'Oh, yes, and she proceeded to use it every time he came onto the ward, only she went one further and abbreviated Franklin to Frankie.'

'I'd love to have seen that,' said Benedict with a deep chuckle. 'Children are the greatest levellers, aren't they?'

By this time they'd reached the babies' section of the ward where a care assistant and a nursery nurse were in charge of four tiny patients. The care assistant looked up from changing a nappy.

'Mollie, this is Dr Lawrence,' said Sophie. 'He's our new reg.'

'Hello, Doctor.' Mollie Seager curiously eyed the new registrar before smothering the baby's bottom with cream.

Benedict smiled and nodded. 'How many babies can you take here at any one time?' he asked.

'We have six cots, but they're rarely all full.' It was Sophie who replied as Benedict bent over one of the cots and lifted a baby up into his arms. It was a little boy of about a year old who had been standing in one corner of the cot, crying lustily and gripping the bars.

'Now, what's all this noise about, young man?' Benedict settled the toddler into the crook of his arm where he promptly made a grab for the stethoscope in the doctor's top pocket. Miraculously the baby's cries grew less until they finally dwindled to a few sobs. As Benedict and Sophie resumed their tour of the nursery section, with the toddler still in the registrar's arms, the sobs turned to smiles and finally to chuckles of delight.

When they returned to Mollie several minutes later, the care assistant took the baby from Benedict. 'You do realize, Dr Lawrence,' she said with an admonishing look, 'that we won't be able to do anything with him now, and there's no way he's going to go back into that cot. Are you, Jamie?'

When the baby merely gurgled in response, Benedict laughed and said, 'Ah, a cuddle never hurt anyone in my experience.' Growing serious, he said, 'What's he in for?'

'Circumcision,' replied Mollie. 'Two days ago.'

'In that case, he needs all the cuddles he can get,' the registrar replied darkly.

They moved on after that, with Sophie showing him the other areas of the ward—the parents' quarters, and the cubicles for the older children each with its own bed, locker, chair and selection of toys, books and posters, the play area where they found that Harry had grown bored with the Lego and was playing with a toy garage, the two isolation wards, the bathrooms and toilets, sluice and kitchen, and finally the nurses' station and offices.

'Well, I think that's about it,' said Sophie, glancing at her watch.

'Thank you,' Benedict said. He spoke quietly as if he really meant it. 'It makes such a difference if someone takes the trouble to show you round. Usually we doctors are just left to muddle through as best we can.' He paused, his gaze meeting hers. 'But I mustn't keep you—you have an admission to do.'

'Yes, I do,' Sophie agreed, then quickly looked away. There was something a little disconcerting about his gaze. 'Would you like to wait in the office? I shouldn't think Sister will be too long.'

'No.' He shook his head. 'I have to meet Mr Crowley-Smith in a few minutes. But, no doubt, I shall be back with him for his rounds.'

'OK, see you then.'

'Yes, see you.' He smiled and moved away.

He really was very nice, thought Sophie as she hurried back down the ward in the opposite direction, and he seemed good with the children as well. She had barely entered the corridor when the lift doors opened and a woman and two young children stepped out.

'Hello,' said Sophie moving forward to greet them. 'Mrs Stewart?'

'Yes.' The woman nodded nervously, her eyes darting around.

Sophie looked down at the children who were gazing up at her open-mouthed. One was a little girl of about four, the other a boy who was a year or two older. 'And you,' she said, looking at the girl, 'must be Chloe. Am I right?'

It was the boy who answered. 'Yes,' he said, 'she's Chloe and I'm Sam. She's going to have an…an…op'ration.'

'I'm not,' said the little girl, her eyes filling with tears. 'I'm going home.'

'Tell you what, Chloe.' Sophie crouched down in front of the child so that their eyes were on the same level. 'Why don't we go and see what toys they have in there?' She inclined her head in the direction of the ward behind her, but the little girl seemed far from being persuaded.

'Come on, Chloe,' said her mother in growing embarrassment. 'We mustn't waste the nurse's time—they're very busy people, you know.'

'It's all right,' said Sophie. 'At the moment my time is all for Chloe.'

'Have you got an Action Man in there?' asked Sam, standing on tiptoe and trying to see into the ward.

'There might be,' Sophie replied. 'I'm sure I seem to remember seeing one somewhere.' She stood up. 'Shall we go and look?'

'Come on, Chloe.' Sam took hold of his sister's hand and began drawing her towards the ward. 'Let's go and see.'

Together they entered the ward, where Sophie led the way straight to the play area. Harry had abandoned the garage by this time but three other children were now in the area, playing with other toys. They all eyed the newcomers suspiciously until Sophie said, 'This is Chloe, who has come to join us for a little while, and this is her brother, Sam, who I'm sure will be visiting her. I want you to welcome them and show them where all the toys are kept.' Immediately the children made room for Chloe and Sam. Sophie turned to Chloe's mother. 'It doesn't take long usually—not after they've seen the toys. Now, I understand it's been arranged for you to stay here with Chloe?'

'Yes, that *is* all right, isn't it?' Mrs Stewart looked anxious. 'She's a very nervous child, you see. My husband is coming in to visit this evening and he'll take Sam home with him.

Normally Sam would have been at school to-day but his school's closed—a training day, I think, for the staff.'

'It'll probably help Chloe to have Sam here for the rest of the day,' Sophie replied. 'It will help her to settle in more quickly. Now, while they're playing, maybe we could complete Chloe's admission form. Let's go into the office—it'll be quieter in there.'

The office was in full view of the play area and Sophie saw that Chloe could look up from her play from time to time and satisfy herself that her mother was still there.

'Most of these are just routine questions,' said Sophie after she'd checked on Chloe's vaccinations, immunisations and antitetanus injections, making sure they were all up to date. 'I do need to know if she's had any operations in the past.' When Mrs Stewart shook her head Sophie carried swiftly on to the next question. 'What about illnesses?'

'She had chickenpox last year after Sam caught it at school.'

'Anything else?'

'No, I don't think so—just the usual coughs and colds.'

'Any allergies?' Sophie glanced up. 'No? Good. What about any special needs?'

'Special needs?' Mrs Stewart looked faintly alarmed.

'Yes,' Sophie said, 'with diet or anything else?'

'Oh, no.' Mrs Stewart paused. 'Although I suppose there are some things she won't eat. And there's one other thing—but I'm sure you won't want to know about that...'

'Believe me, Mrs Stewart, we do,' Sophie replied. 'If it has anything to do with Chloe's well-being we want to know about it.'

'Well, she won't eat eggs at the moment in any shape or form and she doesn't like greens. I do try with her but she simply refuses to eat them.'

Sophie duly noted these dislikes on the form then, glancing up again when Mrs Stewart remained silent, she said, 'And the other thing?'

'She has a piece of rag...' Mrs Stewart looked embarrassed. 'It gets quite disgusting at times because she hates it to be washed— she says it smells wrong if it's washed—but she takes it everywhere with her. It's a piece of an old patchwork quilt...'

'That's exactly the sort of thing we need to know,' said Sophie with a smile. 'If it's something that gives comfort to Chloe we need to know about it, especially at a time when she may be distressed because everything is new or frightening to her. Speaking of which, does she have any particular fears or worries?'

'She doesn't like the dark. I leave a small nightlight on at night.'

'Well, you need have no worries on that score because there's always a dim light burning on the ward at night—and you won't be far away. Now, let's see, what else is there?' Sophie ran her eye down the form. 'Oh, yes, what is your religion?'

'Well, we don't really go to church...'

'Is Chloe baptised?'

'Oh, yes, we had a lovely christening service for both her and Sam.'

'So was this in the Church of England?'

'Yes.'

'That's fine. That's all we need to know,' said Sophie as she wrote 'C of E' in the space provided. 'Now, do you have any questions that you'd like to ask me?'

'Yes.' Mrs Stewart looked anxious again. 'About the operation itself.' When Sophie nodded she carried on. 'Is it tomorrow morning?'

'Yes, it will be. A doctor will come and see Chloc a little later and will talk to you about her hernia repair, then the anaesthetist also will be along and will answer any questions you may have.'

'What about when she goes down to the theatre—will I have to go with her?'

'If you wish to, but you'll only go as far as the anaesthetics room.'

'I know this sounds awful, but I'm not sure if I can do that.' Mrs Stewart began nervously twisting her hands together.

'It doesn't sound awful at all. Many parents don't feel they can face that. Don't worry about it,' said Sophie patiently. 'Chloe will be very drowsy by then from her pre-med—in fact, some children are actually asleep at that point—but, whatever, she won't really know too much that's going on.' Sophie stood up. 'What I'd like to do now is to go and fetch Chloe and show her to her bed then I need to do a few observations.'

'What do you mean?' Mrs Stewart frowned.

'I need to check her temperature and pulse and blood pressure, just simple things like that.'

'Oh, I see.' The woman looked relieved then the frown was back as she said, 'Do you have to do a blood test?'

'Yes, I'm afraid we do.'

'My husband said you would…' Her hands began to twist again.

'Don't worry—we do try to make it as trauma-free as we can for young children. Come on, let's go and get Chloe.'

When they reached the play area they found Chloe playing with the Lego, and Sam and another boy investigating the contents of a toy doctor's bag.

'Chloe,' said Sophie as the little girl looked up, 'I thought you might like to come and see where you're going to sleep.'

'I want to see,' said Sam quickly.

'That's all right,' Sophie replied. 'You can both come.'

They were halfway down the ward when they met Andrea Golding, who was Sophie's friend and the other staff nurse on duty that morning. Andrea had just taken a young patient down to the renal unit for a session of kidney dialysis.

'Hello.' Andrea smiled at Sophie then looked down at Chloe. 'Who do we have here?'

'This is Chloe,' Sophie replied. 'She's joining us for a few days.'

'And I'm Sam,' piped up her brother.

'Well, hello, Sam,' said Andrea with a chuckle. She was about to move on down the ward when she paused and in a low voice said to Sophie, 'Old Crowley-Smith is on his way up.'

'Already!' Sophie rolled her eyes. 'Sister isn't back from her meeting yet.'

'He'll just have to make do with us, won't he?' said Andrea with a grin.

'Absolutely,' Sophie replied. 'Oh, Andrea,' she said, 'have you seen the new reg yet?'

'No, have you?' asked Andrea curiously.

'Yes, he came up here earlier for a look around.'

'What's he like?'

'Wait and see,' said Sophie.

'Oh, no. Not that bad.' Andrea gave a groan. 'That last one was awful.'

'Like I say, just wait and see.' Sophie smiled and carried on down the ward with the Stewart family in tow.

'This will be your bed, Chloe.' Sophie stopped at the cubicle that had been reserved for Chloe. 'And this is your locker.' She opened the locker door and pulled open the drawer. 'What I was wondering...' she turned to the little girl who was clinging to her mother's jacket '...was whether you would like to unpack your bag yourself, then you could put your things away. That way you'll know exactly where to find everything.'

Still Chloe hung back and in the end it was Sam who took the initiative. 'Come on, Chloe,' he said, taking the black holdall out of his mother's hand and hauling it up onto the bed. 'I'll help you.' He unzipped the bag and took out a pink sponge bag and a hairbrush. With that, Chloe stepped forward and dived into the bag herself, pulling out her pyjamas, dressing-gown, slippers, a change of day clothes and a large rag doll whose name turned out to be Rosie.

'I'm really glad you brought Rosie,' said Sophie, as Sam passed the other items to his sister who was crouched down in front of the locker.

'Why?' asked Chloe suspiciously, looking over her shoulder.

'Because we can get her ready and she can have an operation just like you!'

Chloe's eyes widened but as Sophie laid Rosie on the bed and exposed her smooth pink tummy she quickly grew interested. For the next few minutes Sophie painstakingly explained and demonstrated to Chloe, using the rag doll, what would happen during the operation to repair her hernia. 'And this,' she said, 'is where Rosie will have a dressing when she comes back.'

'What's a dressing?' asked Chloe.

'It's a plaster, isn't it, miss?' said Sam excitedly. 'I had one when I fell off the school wall.'

'That's right, Sam,' Sophie replied, 'although in Chloe's and Rosie's cases it may well be a gauze pad held in place by strips of plaster.'

'Will there be much blood?' asked Sam with obvious relish.

'Sam!' said his mother warningly.

'There may be some,' said Sophie truthfully, 'but not very much. Now, we have a few little jobs to do on Rosie and Chloe.'

'What jobs?' asked Chloe fearfully.

'Well, for a start, we need to see how warm you are, then we have to put a cuff on your arm and blow up that little rubber ball.' She indicated the sphygmomanometer on a shelf above Chloe's locker. 'After that,' she went on when she had the children's attention again, 'I shall want to see how much you weigh and how tall you are—and Rosie, of course.'

'Well, this looks a very interesting little group, I have to say.' At the sound of a male voice, Sophie turned and looked up sharply to find Mr Crowley-Smith the consultant paediatrician, together with Sister Bailey who must have just arrived back on the ward from her meeting, two of his house doctors—Samir Youssef and Tess Hewlett—and his new paediatric registrar, Benedict Lawrence. 'Maybe, Staff Nurse Quentin,' the consultant went on, 'you can tell us what's going on here.'

'Of course.' Sophie straightened up, suddenly very aware of Benedict and that he was watching her closely—a half-smile on his face.

She was also aware that Andrea, who had moved back into the main body of the ward, was standing in a cubicle opposite Chloe's and appeared to be watching the proceedings with great interest.

Taking a deep breath, Sophie began to explain. 'We have a young patient here, Mr Crowley-Smith, who has just been admitted. She's on your list for tomorrow for a femoral hernia repair. Her name is Chloe Stewart, and this is her mother and her brother Sam. Chloe has just unpacked her belongings and is settling into the ward. I was about to carry out the routine observations.'

'I see. And what is the significance of this young lady?' As he spoke the consultant leaned forward and touched the rag doll.

It was Chloe who answered his question— a red-faced, slightly indignant Chloe, who stepped forward and gazed up at the tall man who stood before her, his hands clasped behind his back in what was his habitual stance, and with the fresh white rosebud which had become his own personal trade mark tucked into his buttonhole. 'This is Rosie,' she said in a loud, clear voice. 'She's got a bad tummy as well as me. Nurse is going to make her better, aren't you, Nurse?' It was the most Chloe had said since she'd arrived and it brought a smile to the faces of all those watching.

'I'm very pleased to hear it. Well done, Nurse Quentin. Keep up the good work.' Mr Crowley-Smith nodded and rocked slightly back and forth on his heels. 'I'll see you later, Chloe—and Rosie, of course.' With that he moved on, his entourage following him, but as Benedict passed Sophie he half turned and winked at her.

CHAPTER TWO

'WELL, I have to say, he's certainly an improvement on the last one—in fact, on the last three or so, now I come to think of it,' said Andrea with a little sniff.

'The thing is, he seems to be nice as well,' replied Sophie. 'The really good-looking ones are often so full of themselves that they're really unbearable.' It was much later and the two girls were relaxing in the staff canteen over sandwiches and glasses of fresh orange juice. Inevitably their conversation had come around to the new paediatric registrar.

'Do you know anything about him?' asked Andrea curiously as she bit into her sandwich.

'Like what?' said Sophie with a grin. 'His medical qualifications, do you mean?'

'I was thinking more on the lines of whether or not he's married,' replied Andrea crisply.

'Now, how did I guess that was what you were thinking?' Sophie laughed then shook her head. 'Sorry, haven't a clue—we didn't get on to anything like that.'

'Bet he is, or at least spoken for—a good-looking guy like that.'

'Oh, I don't know—you could well be in with a chance if you play your cards right.'

'Huh—fat chance.' Andrea pulled a face. 'If I remember rightly, it was you he was looking at all the time and you he winked at just before he left the ward.'

'Only because he doesn't know any better,' replied Sophie.

'So, how *is* Miles?' Andrea leaned back in her chair and eyed Sophie speculatively.

'He's very well, at least as far as I know, or he was a couple of nights ago when I spoke to him.'

'When's he coming down again?'

'I'm not sure.' Sophie frowned. 'He's in Manchester at the moment and next week he has to go up to Durham so I doubt if I'll be seeing him for a while.'

'Any chance of him moving down here?'

'That would be marvellous.' Sophie sighed. 'And I do live in hopes. The problem is his father—Miles does feel he needs to keep an eye on him.'

'Oh, yes, I forgot about his father. What is it that's wrong with him?'

'Parkinson's disease,' Sophie replied.

'And doesn't Miles have any brothers or sisters who could help out?'

'No. Unfortunately he's the only one. I'm really not sure how we're going to work things out.'

'You'll work it out.' Andrea sighed and stood up. 'Love will find a way. I'd better get back. Michael will be ready to come back from his dialysis.'

'And I've got some reports to do before I go off duty.' Sophie pushed her plate away and also rose to her feet.

'How's that new little girl settling in?' asked Andrea a few minutes later as they left the canteen and made their way back to the ward.

'Chloe? Oh, I think she'll be fine. She was very nervous at first but I think it's helped, having her mother and her brother stay with her.'

An hour later Sophie finished her reports and briefly, before going off duty, went back onto the ward. Chloe and Sam were sitting in the rest area with their mother, who was reading them a story. Harry had also joined the little group and was curled up in an armchair next to Mrs Stewart, listening to the adventures of Paddington Bear. Satisfied that all was well, Sophie crept away, and as the new shift came on duty she hurried to the staffroom to change. Moments later she was heading for the car park.

The weather had been mostly mild that winter but now there was definitely a chill in the air, and as Sophie crossed the car park she pulled up her collar as the same keen breeze that tugged at her hair also whipped up great flurries of dead leaves and tossed them around the hospital grounds.

Unlocking her car, she slipped into the driver's seat, secured her seat belt then started the engine. It was as she pulled out of the car park and onto the path that led down the hill to the main road that she saw the figure ahead of her. He was wearing a long, dark overcoat with the collar turned up, and he had his head down as he battled against the wind, but there was no mistaking who it was. She hesitated.

Should she stop? He quite obviously didn't have transport of his own and it was a fair distance from the hospital into the town. It was also a well-known fact that the bus service wasn't as frequent as it might have been.

Sophie had almost caught him up when he slowed his pace and half turned, glancing right at her.

Instinctively she braked, that simple glance of his making her mind up for her. Later she was to wonder, if she'd not stopped that day and had carried right on, whether things would have turned out differently, but at the time all she was aware of was his smile when he realised it was her. Winding down her window, she said, 'Are you going into town?'

'Yes.' Benedict nodded. He looked cold. His eyes were watering and his nose was quite pink.

'I'll give you a lift.' She couldn't fail to notice his grateful expression.

'This is good of you,' he said as he got into the car, slammed the door and fastened his seat belt. 'I swear, that wind is straight from Siberia.'

'Don't you have any transport?' she asked curiously as she drew away.

'My car's gone in for repair. You don't realise how much you rely on a car until you haven't got it.'

'Where do you live?' Sophie was suddenly very aware of him sitting beside her, just as she had been on the ward when she'd shown him around, and later when he'd accompanied the consultant on his rounds.

'I've just got myself a flat. It's down by the river in a new complex.'

'Is it one of those on the old brewery site?' She threw him an interested glance.

'That's right.' He looked faintly surprised that she should know. 'I was in hospital accommodation before but it was far from satisfactory. That sort of thing was fine when I was a student and even later as a houseman I didn't mind, but I guess as you get older you value your privacy and a certain amount of peace and quiet.' He laughed. 'Heavens, I sound like my father!'

'I know what you mean,' said Sophie with a laugh. 'I used to live in the nurses' home when I was a student, and that lifestyle was fine then, with parties nearly every night, but I'm not sure I could cope with that now.'

'So where is home?'

'Actually, at the moment I'm living with my parents, believe it or not. But it's only a temporary arrangement. The lease ran out on the flat I had and I'm looking for another one.'

'Your parents live here in Westbury?' He sounded surprised.

'Yes, my father's a GP in a small practice on the far side of the town.'

'So you're a local. Have you always lived in Westbury?'

'Apart from when I was doing my training in London. How about you?' She threw him a sidelong glance. 'Where is your family home?'

'Norfolk,' Benedict replied. 'My parents still live there.'

'What brought you all the way down here to Hampshire?'

'The job. I'd heard of Mr Crowley-Smith and had read many of his articles in the medical journals. When I knew he was looking for a registrar I applied immediately, not really believing I had a hope in hell of getting the job. I even thought I'd fluffed the interview. I simply couldn't believe it when I had the letter saying that I had been successful.'

By this time they'd reached the town. Everywhere there were signs of the rapidly approaching festive season, from the brightly decorated shops to the huge Christmas tree in the main square beside the church.

'I wish the onset of Christmas would just stop for a while and allow me to get organised,' said Sophie as she carefully negotiated the one-way traffic system. 'It seems to have crept up on me this year almost without me noticing.'

'Me, too,' said Benedict. 'But, then, that's nothing new. It has a habit of doing that every year if I'm really honest. I'm one of those people who posts their cards at the last possible moment and is actually buying presents just before the shops close on Christmas Eve.'

'I don't think I'm quite that bad—but I know what you mean.' She paused as she drew up at a set of traffic lights then, as they changed to green and the stream of traffic drew off again, she said, 'Will you go home to Norfolk for Christmas?'

He shook his head. 'No, not this year. I've volunteered for duty. I think it's only fair to let those with young families have the time off.'

'Me, too,' Sophie agreed.

'I shall probably go home for New Year,' he added thoughtfully, and Sophie found herself wondering if there was someone he would want to see in the New Year with.

By this time they had driven right through the town and under the flyover, taking the road beside the river. Sophie knew the site of Clifton's Brewery—it had stood empty and derelict for many years but had recently been taken over by a property developer. The resulting complex had been tastefully renovated, using the shell of the old building, thereby making sure the ensuing development was in keeping with the surroundings.

'So whereabouts are you?' Sophie slowed the car and peered through the windscreen. Although it was still only mid-afternoon, the light was already fading and the sky over the river had flushed to a dull crimson.

'Just here.' Benedict indicated to the left where glimpses of a paved courtyard were visible beneath a bricked archway which bore the sign CLIFTON COURT. 'You can drop me here then you'll be able to turn round.'

Sophie brought the car to a halt and looked up at the windows of the building above the archway. Each window had its own wrought-iron balcony. 'They look really nice apartments,' she said slowly. 'I made enquiries about them but I gather they were all snapped up pretty quickly.'

'That's true,' he agreed. He paused. 'Actually, though,' he went on after a moment, 'there's one on my floor that's still vacant. Apparently the sale fell through at the last minute and it's going back on the market. Would you still be interested?'

'I could be,' Sophie replied. 'Normally this sort of thing would be way out of my price range, but my grandmother died recently and left me some money.'

'In that case, why not come and have a look round mine?' said Benedict casually. 'I imagine they're all quite similar.'

'Well, I don't know…' She hesitated.

'Come on. What have you got to lose?'

Sophie switched off the engine and un-clipped her seat belt. Benedict was right—what did she have to lose just by having a look at the place? If it wasn't what she wanted or she didn't like it, she only had to say it wasn't suitable. On the other hand, as she climbed out of the car she felt a sudden tingle of excitement and she felt that this could be exactly what she was looking for.

After locking the car, she followed Benedict through the archway and into the courtyard. Like those on the outside, the windows over-looking the courtyard with its pink and grey paving stones all seemed to have neat black balconies.

'I've tried to imagine this in the summer,' said Benedict. 'You know, all terracotta pots packed with geraniums.'

'Very continental,' said Sophie with a laugh, waiting as Benedict produced a card and in-serted it in a slot in a panel alongside the main entrance. As the door slid open they stepped into the foyer.

'We'll take the stairs instead of the lift,' he said. 'That way you'll see a bit more of the place. I'm on the second floor.'

Together they climbed the stairs and at each turn in the stairwell large windows afforded glimpses of the courtyard below. On the second floor they turned into a corridor with many closed doors on either side. Benedict eventually stopped at one and inserted his card in the lock. As the door swung open he stepped back and with a flourish indicated for Sophie to precede him into an L-shaped hallway. He closed the door then brushed past her and led the way into the sitting-room.

Her first impression was that the room was too dark, then she realized that the blinds were drawn. With a muttered exclamation Benedict strode across the room and released the catch of the blinds, and the last of the day's light stole into the room.

Sophie stood in the centre of the room and looked around her. It was plainly furnished with light wood, neutral fabrics and biscuit-coloured upholstery in soft leather. The lamps and hi-fi equipment were black and ornaments were at a minimum, with just two pieces of bleached driftwood, one jade vase and a single picture of some exotic oriental landscape. It was essentially a man's room.

'It's quite simple really,' he said, stopping to look around as if he also were seeing the room for the first time. 'Through here…' he went back into the hall and opened a second door '…is the bedroom.' Sophie joined him.

This room was decorated and furnished in shades of blue, with the lightest shade for the walls, drifting through the range, darkening with curtains and carpet and ending with bed covers of French navy beneath a crisp white cotton bedspread with a cut-out design.

The room was tidy, the only hint of its occupant being a small clock and a paperback thriller beside the bed and a pair of faded blue jeans folded over the back of the room's only chair. For some reason the sight of the jeans, so ordinary yet somehow intimate, affected Sophie, although she would have been at a loss to say why, and she looked quickly away.

They moved into the hall again and Benedict closed the bedroom door. 'The bathroom is in here.' He pushed open another door and Sophie looked into an immaculate, white-tiled bathroom. 'And over here…' he crossed the hall again '…is the kitchen-diner.' This was another L-shaped room, well fitted in pine and equipped with every labour-saving device, and had a small but adequate dining area.

'So, what do you think?' Benedict said as they moved back into the main room. 'I can't see that the other flat could be that different.'

'I think it's lovely,' Sophie replied. 'In fact, it could be just what I'm looking for. I think I'll go and see the agents tomorrow.'

'Why wait until tomorrow?' said Benedict. 'I should see them today if you're interested. As you said yourself, these flats have been snapped up very quickly.'

'In that case, maybe I will...that is, if you think you could stand having me as a neighbour...'

'Oh,' he replied lazily, 'I can't see that that would be too much of a problem.'

Briefly Sophie allowed her gaze to meet his and what she saw there was amusement in those rather curious eyes of his, that the greenish flecks shone and seemed more numerous than before and that the little creases were back around his eyes.

For a moment she didn't know quite what else to say and then she had the sudden, ridiculous, almost overwhelming desire to sink down onto that soft leather sofa with Benedict beside her.

Instead, she gave herself a little mental shake in an effort to pull herself together. 'Well,' she said at last, only too aware that her voice not only sounded breathless but also shook a little, 'I'd best be going...'

'Oh,' he said, the amusement dying from his eyes, 'do you have to? Couldn't you stay awhile? Have a drink? Or a cup of tea maybe?'

She had to fight the urge to say yes, for suddenly she wanted to stay—more than anything she wanted to stay—but something inside her was telling her she shouldn't. He was far too attractive, far too nice for her to cultivate any leanings in that particular direction. 'No, really,' she said at last. 'I must be going, but thank you, thank you very much for showing me around.'

'It's no problem, I assure you.' The amusement was back in his eyes. 'After all, one good turn deserves another.'

They had reached the door by now. 'One good turn?' She paused.

''Yes, today—you took the trouble to show me around the ward. Like I said, there aren't many who bother to do that.'

'Oh, that was nothing.' Sophie shrugged, suddenly embarrassed.

'It wasn't ''nothing'' to me. New place. New home. New job. You know what it's like—you're glad for any kind word or gesture. And if that wasn't enough, you also gave me a lift home.' Benedict opened the door. 'I'll come down with you.'

'Oh, there's no need...'

'Nonsense. It's the least I can do.'

In silence they walked to the stairs. Desperate for something to say to break the silence, which, to Sophie at least, had somehow become disconcerting, she said, 'Do you think you'll like it here in Westbury?'

'Oh, yes, I think so,' he replied. 'I suppose it's my sort of town, similar to my own home town really.'

'And St Winifred's?'

'Yes, it has the right feel about it, and I'm more than pleased to have the opportunity to be working with Franklin Crowley-Smith.'

As they walked out of the building and into the courtyard the wind whipped through the archway and Sophie thrust her hands into her pockets and nestled deeper into her coat. Benedict walked beside her all the way to the car, where he held the door open for her as she climbed in.

'Thanks,' she said, looking up at him. 'I'll see you tomorrow. Are you on the same shift?'

'Yes.' He nodded. 'And you?'

'Yes.'

'I'll see you then. Bye, Sophie.'

'Bye.'

As she drove away, even before she looked in her rear-view mirror, she knew Benedict was watching her. Standing silhouetted in the archway, he stood there in his dark greatcoat, the collar turned up against the chill wind.

It was dark by the time she reached home, but the house—a huge, red-brick Victorian building, complete with gables and turrets— was, as ever, ablaze with lights. The entire ground floor was given over to the medical practice of her father, Richard Quentin, and his partner, Henry Frost, while the upstairs had been converted into living accommodation for the two doctors and their families.

After parking her car in its usual space at the rear of the building, alongside the dark mass of rhododendron and hydrangea bushes that lined the drive, Sophie let herself in at the private entrance. Surgeries were still in progress and the front of the house was a hive of activity, with patients coming and going and the staff—harassed at the end of a long day—endeavouring to sort out their problems.

Nimbly Sophie climbed the stairs to their apartment where she found her mother in the kitchen, preparing vegetables for the evening meal. 'Hi, Mum,' she said, giving her a peck on the cheek.

'Hello, dear. Had a good day?' Her mother always said that, and usually Sophie gave one of a few stock answers, depending on what her day had been like. Today, however, she found herself considering before she answered. Today had been different. Very different. Her mother must have noticed the slight hesitation in the line of their usual patter because she turned from the sink and threw her daughter a keen glance. 'Sophie?' she said. 'Is everything all right, dear?'

'Oh, yes,' Sophie replied at last. 'Yes, everything's fine. It's just that today seems to have been different, that's all.'

'Oh? In what way?' Patricia Quentin began wiping her hands.

'Well,' said Sophie, 'for a start, we have a new registrar on the unit.'

'What's this one like?' Her mother, herself once a nurse, was well used to stories of previous registrars and consultants, and always liked a good gossip with her daughter about the staff at St Winifred's.

'So far he seems very nice,' Sophie replied reflectively, 'although, of course, it's early days yet. But one thing that's happened—' a note of excitement crept into her voice '—is that I think he may have found me a flat. I think I'd better explain that,' she said with a chuckle as she caught sight of her mother's look of astonishment. 'You see, I gave him a lift home—the registrar, I mean, whose name by the way is Benedict Lawrence. He has an apartment down by the river—you know, one of those on the site of Clifton's Brewery.

'Anyway, I happened to tell him I was looking for a new flat and he said there was just
one left because its sale had fallen through. I
went in with him and he showed me his apartment. Honestly, Mum, it was lovely—just the
sort of place I would love. I called into
Marshalls, the estate agent in the square, on
the way home and got the details. Here, look.'
She rummaged in her bag and passed the details of the apartment across the kitchen table
to her mother.

Patricia Quentin who, with her pale blonde
hair and deep blue eyes, looked like an older
version of her daughter, sat down, put on her
reading glasses and carefully began to study
the brochure.

'It would, of course, normally be out of the
question on my salary,' said Sophie, not waiting for her mother to finish reading, 'but now,
thanks to Grandma Quentin's legacy, it would
be within my reach.'

'You would buy this time, rather than rent?'
asked her mother, without taking her eyes off
the brochure.

'Yes,' Sophie replied slowly, 'I think I
would. The legacy has changed everything. I

was talking to Dad about it the other day and he said he felt it would be a sensible invest-ment for me to use some of the money to buy my own property.'

'And what about Miles in all this?' Patricia lowered the brochure and looked up at her daughter over the top of her spectacles.

'Miles?' Sophie paused enquiringly.

'Don't you and he have any long-term plans?'

'Well, yes, eventually I hope we'll be able to be together—of course I do—but at the mo-ment Miles is in Manchester and can't leave his father for too long. If we do get together at some point in the future I can always sell the flat, and then presumably we'll buy a place between us.'

Her mother was silent for a while, reading again. 'He phoned earlier,' she said at last, without looking up. 'He thought you'd be home.'

'Oh?' Sophie looked up quickly. 'Did he leave any message?'

'Not really. We had a little chat then I said you'd probably ring him back later.'

'Yes, I will. Of course I will.' Sophie left her mother sitting at the kitchen table and slowly made her way to her room, but she was at a loss to explain why the feeling of euphoria she'd felt earlier after leaving Benedict, and which had persisted throughout her visit to the estate agent and her journey home, had quite suddenly disappeared, leaving her feeling very flat.

CHAPTER THREE

MILES answered his mobile phone on the tenth ring. 'Hello?'

'Oh,' said Sophie with a laugh, 'you are there. I was about to hang up.'

'I was just helping Dad to the bathroom.'

'Oh, I'm sorry. Shall I ring back?'

'No, it's OK. He's back in his room again now.'

'I thought perhaps you were out on the road somewhere.'

'No,' he replied. 'I was earlier when I rang. I spoke to your mum.'

'Yes, I know. She said.'

'You were late. I thought you would have been home by then.'

'Yes,' she agreed, detecting, she thought, a faintly accusing note in his voice. 'I was late, but you just wait until I tell you what I was doing.'

'Oh?'

She knew she had his interest and she smiled to herself. 'I was looking at a flat.'

'Really?' There was no mistaking his interest now. Life had been quite difficult on his visits since she'd lost her last flat and had been forced to move back to her parents' home.

'It's really nice, Miles. I'm sure you'll like it.'

'Where is it exactly?'

'Well, remember that day we walked down by the river? When it was so hot?'

'How could I forget it?' His voice softened.

'Yes. Well, it's in that new complex they were building. You know, the old brewery site?'

'Yes—but were those apartments to let?'

'I'm thinking of buying this time, Miles.'

'Is that a wise move, do you think?'

'Yes,' she replied. 'I think it will be a good investment now that I have my legacy.' There was silence at the other end of the line. 'Miles?' she said. 'Are you still there?'

'Yes.'

'What's wrong?'

'I wanted us to be looking for something that we could buy together.'

'We may still do that, but later. Honestly, Miles, there's no hurry and you can't just leave your father, can you?'

'I know.' She heard his sigh. 'It's just that I'm tired of us being apart. I want to be with you, Sophie.'

'I know,' she said gently. 'And I want us to be together as well. It just isn't quite the right time yet, that's all. But just think how much easier it will be when you come down now. No more willing Mum and Dad to go out.' She laughed. 'Speaking of which, just when will you be down again?'

'Well, I've got all northern towns to do for the next couple of weeks, but after that I reckon I could justify a trip south, maybe the weekend before Christmas.'

They had already agreed that Christmas itself would be out of the question, with Sophie working at the hospital and Miles with his father to care for.

'That weekend will be wonderful,' said Sophie, 'because it's the staff Christmas party on the Saturday.'

'Do you think you'll have this flat by then?'

'I don't know. I've only just been to the agents. You know how long these things take.'

'True,' he agreed. 'But it must help, not having to arrange a mortgage.'

'Yes,' she agreed, 'I suppose there is that. We'll just have to see how things go.'

They chatted for a while longer until Miles had to go following a call from his father and after promising to ring her again in a few days.

She replaced the receiver and sat for a while on her bed, reflecting on their conversation. Miles had sounded rather tense—no doubt he was finding it stressful, trying to care for his father and arranging for someone from Social Services to do so when he was away. Miles was a medical representative for Panasonium Laboratories, a large pharmaceutical company. Mostly his territory was in the north, but a year previously he'd come south to a large pharmaceutical convention which had been held in the boardroom at St Winifred's.

Some of the nursing staff had been chosen to attend the lectures at the convention. On the second day Sophie had gone and that was where she and Miles had first met. He'd come and sat beside her in the staff canteen and had introduced himself. She'd immediately been struck by his good looks, his charming manner and the quickness of his wit, and when later they'd got up to return to the conference hall she'd made no protest when he'd suggested they sit together for the rest of the lectures.

He'd taken her out to dinner that night, and by the end of the evening they'd known practically everything there had been to know about each other. Sophie had told him all about her background and he'd told her about the difficulties he'd been having, trying to care for his father. He explained that he'd even moved out of his own flat and back into the family home because it had been more practical.

When the conference was over he promised he would phone and that he would come down again to see her. Within a few weeks he'd managed to include some southern towns in his territory, giving him a legitimate reason for travelling down as far as Westbury.

Sophie looked forward to his visits, although as time went on she sometimes found herself wondering if their relationship was going anywhere. He told her he loved her and that he wanted them to be together, but there were times when he seemed distant, evasive almost, and Sophie was left wondering. Maybe things would be better once she had her own place again. She brightened up at the thought and with a renewed tingle of excitement she reached for the estate agent's brochure.

'Come on, Chloe, we're going to dress you and Rosie in these special white nightgowns.'

'Why?' asked Chloe.

'Because it will be easier for the doctor to do your operation.'

'Will it be that doctor we saw yesterday?'

'Yes, it will, and Dr Lawrence will be helping him.'

'They'll be busy, won't they—what with Rosie as well?'

'Yes,' Sophie agreed, 'they will.'

'What's wrong with that little baby who keeps crying?' Chloe swivelled round on her bed to look down into Teletubby land where the cries of a young baby could be heard all over the ward.

'He's very poorly,' said Sophie.

'Will the doctor make him better?' asked Chloe anxiously.

'Oh, yes,' Sophie replied firmly.

'Which doctor? Dr Lawrence or the other one—Mr...Crowley—?'

'Chloe!' It was her mother who intervened. 'Don't keep asking questions. Nurse Sophie is very busy this morning.'

'It's all right.' Sophie looked up quickly. 'Really, it is. I don't mind. I'm just pleased she's settled down so well.' She paused then, looking keenly at Mrs Stewart who looked tired and drawn, she said, 'How about you? Did you sleep?'

Chloe's mother shook her head. 'No, hardly at all. I kept thinking I'd heard Chloe, and even after I'd satisfied myself that she was all right I couldn't get back to sleep. I just lay there for hours, tossing and turning and thinking about today.'

'She *will* be all right, you know.' Gently Sophie put a reassuring hand on the other woman's arm.

'Yes, I'm sure she will. It's just us mothers—I guess there's nothing on earth that will stop us worrying.' She paused, appearing to hesitate. 'I've been thinking about what you were saying about going down to Theatre with

Chloe... And I think I will go after all, if that's all right.'

'Of course it is,' replied Sophie. 'And if I can arrange it, I'll try and make sure that I'm the one to accompany you down there. Then you'll be able to come back here to the ward with me. By the time you've had a cup of tea you'll find it'll practically be time for Chloe to come back.'

'Thanks.' Mrs Stewart blinked rapidly. 'You've been so good and I know Chloe thinks of you as her own special nurse.' They both looked down at Chloe who was fussing over her doll.

'I need to do a few more routine checks,' said Sophie.

'To see how warm I am?' asked Chloe, looking up.

'That's one of them, yes,' replied Sophie with a laugh as she unpinned the badge that Chloe had been wearing on her pyjamas to inform people she wasn't to have anything to eat or drink. 'We'll just pin this onto your gown for the time being and you must make sure that no one gives any food to Rosie.'

Chloe giggled. 'Rosie doesn't really eat.'

'Doesn't she?' said Sophie. 'I thought she did. Now, the other thing we have to do is to give you both some medicine.'

'Yuck, I don't like medicine.' Chloe pulled a face.

'You'll like this,' said Sophie. 'It tastes of oranges.'

'I'm going to be a nurse when I grow up,' said Chloe a few minutes later as she snuggled down in her bed with Rosie. 'And d'you know what? Sam's going to be a doctor—just like Dr Lawrence.'

At the mention of Benedict Sophie's heart gave a funny little leap, and it was at that moment she realised that subconsciously she'd actually been waiting for the registrar to put in an appearance on the ward ever since she'd arrived—only to tell him that she'd been to the estate agent after she'd left him the previous day, of course, not for any other reason. She also wanted to say that she'd reached a decision and had phoned the agent from the ward at nine o'clock as they'd opened.

Leaving Mrs Stewart with her daughter while the pre-med took effect, Sophie made her way back to the nurses' station where she found Sister Bailey, talking to Andrea. They both looked concerned, but before Sophie had a chance to ask what was wrong Sister Bailey turned and looked at her. 'Oh, there you are,' she said. 'I was just telling Andrea I've had a call to say that Antonia Brett is coming in again today. It seems she's had a relapse.'

'Oh, no, she seemed to be doing so well the last time she was here,' said Sophie in dismay. 'Will this mean more surgery?'

'We don't know yet,' Sister Bailey replied. 'More tests will need to be done and I should imagine Mr Crowley-Smith will hold a case conference.' Then, rapidly changing the subject to the case in hand, she said, 'Is Chloe ready for Theatre?'

Sophie nodded. 'Yes, the obs are all complete and she's had her pre-med. And Mum has now decided she will come down to Theatre.'

'Well, that's a turn-around,' said Andrea. 'Yesterday she was adamant she wasn't going down.'

'She had a night of worrying,' said Sophie.

'As they do,' commented Andrea. 'Harry is being discharged after doctors' round this morning,' she added after a moment. 'He told me just now that he doesn't want to go—he wants to stay here and play with the toys.'

'What's with the baby who's just come in?' Sophie glanced down the ward where she could see that Dr Samir Youssef was with the baby and its young parents.

'Febrile convulsions,' replied Andrea. 'The mother went to pieces, apparently, and thought the baby had meningitis. They brought him in to Casualty and he was found to be dehydrated. I'd best get back down there and see if Samir wants any help.' She started as if to go down the ward then she stopped. 'Oh, by the way,' she said, turning back to Sophie, 'did I see the delectable Doctor Lawrence getting into your car yesterday afternoon?'

For some reason, and to her dismay, Sophie felt the colour flood her face.

'It was him, wasn't it? I thought it was, then I thought maybe I was mistaken. What happened?'

'I gave him a lift, that's all. His car was in for repair—'

'And I was only just behind you. Just think, if I'd been a moment earlier it would have

been my car he would have been getting into.'
Andrea gave an exaggerated sigh. 'Honestly,
Sophie, it isn't fair. You get all the luck where
men are concerned, and you don't even need
it because you're already spoken for.' She
paused. 'So where did you drop him off? Did
you go right to his house?'

'Er…yes, I did, as it happens.'

'Where does he live?' demanded Andrea,
when Sophie fell silent. 'Come on, tell us.'

'He has an apartment in that new complex
down by the river.'

'You mean the old brewery site? Wow,
those places must cost a bomb! Mind you, I
guess that wouldn't be a problem, not on a
registrar's salary. Not like us poor old nurses.'

Sophie took a deep breath, feeling some sort
of explanation should be given before Andrea
went too far, but at that moment there was a
buzz of activity at the far end of the ward.

'Oh, Lord, it's the doctors already,' said
Andrea. 'And talk of the devil…'

Benedict was there with the others, in the
centre of the group. To anyone else he would
quite simply have blended in, but to Sophie,
probably because she'd just been talking and

thinking about him, he was the only one she saw. And even as the breath caught in her throat and she watched him, he looked up and saw her. As their gazes met, they locked and held for a long moment until, in utter confusion, she looked away. Then, as Andrea bustled away to the nurses' station to warn Sister that the doctors' round was imminent, Sophie took herself back down the ward to Chloe's bed.

Mrs Stewart looked up as Sophie approached. 'She's asleep,' she said, her gaze moving to the child on the bed who lay with her tangle of dark curls spread across the pillow, her thumb in her mouth and her other arm tightly around Rosie.

'That's good.' Sophie nodded. 'Are you all right?'

'Yes, I'm not so bad now, thanks.'

'A porter will come up and get Chloe later on and we'll both go down to Theater with her.'

'I see the doctors are coming round.' Mrs Stewart glanced at the little group who were clustered around the cubicle next to Chloe's, where Mr Crowley-Smith was talking to

Harry's parents. 'They won't disturb her, will they?' she asked anxiously. 'She's only just dropped off.'

'I shouldn't think so.' Sophie shook her head then straightened up and moved back from the bed as the group moved towards them.

'This is Chloe Stewart,' said Sister Bailey. 'She's on your list for this morning, Mr Crowley-Smith.'

'Ah, yes, the little lady with the femoral hernia. Any problems?'

Sister glanced at her notes. 'Temperature was a little raised last night but nothing apart from that.'

'Is her temperature normal this morning?' asked the consultant.

'Yes, perfectly normal,' Sister replied.

'In that case, we'll proceed. Now, Sister, if that's all, Dr Lawrence and myself need to be on our way down to Theater, otherwise this young lady will be down there before us.' He gave his short bark of a laugh and the others all politely laughed with him, then he nodded towards Mrs Stewart in what was presumably meant to be a reassuring manner.

'The only other thing I need to mention to you at this point,' said Sister as they moved away from Chloe's bed, 'is that Antonia Brett is being admitted this morning.'

The consultant had clasped his hands behind his back as he'd paced down the ward, but at the mention of Antonia's name Sophie saw him pause and look at Sister, his grey eyebrows raised enquiringly.

'It's at her GP's request,' Sister Bailey replied quietly.

'Very well.' Mr Crowley-Smith nodded. 'So be it.'

With that, in a flurry of white coats, the doctors were gone, and all that Sophie was aware of as they left the ward was the briefest of smiles in her direction from the new registrar.

The next half-hour or so was taken up with routine ward tasks of bed-making, bathing and dressings. Sophie found herself avoiding Andrea, knowing her friend would probably bring up the subject of Benedict again and of where he lived. For some reason, and she wasn't quite sure why, she knew she would find it very difficult to tell Andrea that she, too, was in the process of buying one of the apartments at the old brewery site.

Sophie was just returning a dressing trolley to the nurses' station when Jefferson, the paediatric porter, arrived to take Chloe down to Theatre. Jefferson was of West Indian origin, big, cheerful and loved by all in Paediatrics, staff and patients alike.

'Hello, Jefferson.' Sophie smiled in response to his huge grin. 'We're all ready for you. This is Chloe's mother, Mrs Stewart. She'll be going down as far as the anaesthetics room.'

'You coming down, too, Nurse Sophie?' asked Jefferson.

'Oh, yes, Jefferson, I will.'

The porter gave a deep sigh then, looking at Mrs Stewart and with his hand on his heart, he said, 'I wish Nurse Sophie would say that when I ask her out. I've been asking her out for months now and always she says no.'

The laughter that followed diffused any tension there might have been for Mrs Stewart as Chloe, together with her piece of patchwork and Rosie, was lifted onto the trolley. Accompanied by Sophie and her mother, and still fast asleep, she was wheeled out of the ward.

The trek to Theatre was a lengthy one and involved a trip in the lift to a lower floor, then through what seemed like miles of corridors, but, accompanied by Jefferson's cheerful banter, it seemed in no time at all they reached the theatre suite and the trolley was wheeled into the anaesthetics room.

They were met by a theatre staff nurse who officially took over from Sophie, but as Chloe was transferred from the trolley to the couch someone else came into the anaesthetics room. Dressed from head to toe in theatre greens and boots, he was masked, but there was no mistaking Benedict's identity because of the eyes above the mask and once again Sophie felt her heart give that crazy little leap.

By this time Mrs Stewart was beginning to look very nervous indeed. Benedict must have sensed this for, lifting one of Chloe's hands in his, he looked at Sophie and said, 'Time to leave Chloe with us, I think.' As Sophie nodded, he turned to Mrs Stewart. 'Give her a kiss, Mum,' he said, 'and before you know it, we'll have her back in the ward with you.'

Mrs Stewart bent over the sleeping form of her little daughter and gently kissed her cheek. With tears in her eyes she turned and blindly groped her way out of the anaesthetics room.

Sophie glanced at Benedict. 'Go with her,' he said gently as, at that moment, the anesthetist entered the room.

Still there had been no time to tell him of her decision. With a little sigh Sophie hurried after Chloe's mother, whom she found dabbing her eyes with her handkerchief as she waited for her in the corridor outside the anaesthetics room.

'Come on,' said Sophie, taking her arm. 'I think it's time we went and made that cup of tea.'

When they got back to the ward they found that care assistant Mollie Seager had made up Chloe's bed with fresh linen and had placed oxygen and suction beside the bed, together with a vomit bowl and tissues. Sophie then accompanied Mrs Stewart to the parents' recreation area where she made her a cup of tea and left her to relax with a magazine and the radio playing softly beside her.

'Thank you, Nurse.' Mrs Stewart looked up gratefully as Sophie reached the door. 'You've been so kind. I don't know how I would have coped without you.'

'It's all part of the service,' said Sophie.

'So it may be,' said Mrs Stewart, 'but there are some of you who go beyond that and give that little bit extra. You do, so did that porter and so does that Dr Lawrence.'

Something about Mrs Stewart's words and the way she'd said them lifted Sophie's spirits, or maybe it had been the way she'd included Benedict in the same assessment as herself that had done it, Sophie thought as she hurried back to the nurses' station. Not that that should mean anything, of course, she told herself firmly. On the contrary, she really had to stop thinking about Benedict because it seemed that since she'd met him the previous day—hardly possible it had only been a day ago—he had occupied a ridiculously large proportion of her thoughts.

It was probably only the situation over the apartment which had brought this about but, whatever it was, it really had to stop. She had a man in her life, as Andrea kept going to the trouble of reminding her, so she shouldn't be letting thoughts of another fill her mind.

'All well with Chloe?' Sister Bailey's brisk tones interrupted her thoughts and mentally Sophie adjusted her concentration and brought it back to the present.

'Yes, fine,' she replied. 'And Mollie has prepared the cubicle for her return.'

'Did her mother go down with you?' Sister Bailey looked enquiringly over her glasses at Sophie.

'Yes, surprisingly.' Sophie nodded. 'I didn't think she would.'

'Where is she now?'

'In the rest room. I made her a cup of tea.'

'You spoil them,' said Sister, her frown denoting faint disapproval.

Sophie shrugged. 'I try to imagine how I would feel.' She glanced round. 'Has Harry gone?'

'Yes, about ten minutes ago.'

'Oh, I missed him. I wanted to say goodbye,' Sophie protested.

'Well, if you'd come straight here when you got back from Theatre you would have done,' Sister retorted briskly.

'Yes, I suppose so,' said Sophie with a sigh. Then, to change the subject, she said, 'What time is Antonia coming in?'

'Not until after lunch. I want to have a talk with everyone about the care we will be required to give Antonia—and her family,' said Sister. 'It's not going to be easy for anyone because we've all got to know Antonia so well in the last couple of years, but for her family it will be many, many times more distressing.'

'Can nothing else be done at all for her?' asked Sophie.

'Apparently not. At least, not in terms of treatment. She's had all the surgery that was possible and it has been decided that any further chemotherapy would not be beneficial.'

'She and her family are going to need all the support we can give them,' said Sophie.

About an hour later, together with Jefferson, Sophie went down to the theatre suite, where they found Chloe in the recovery room.

'She's all ready to go back,' said the staff nurse on duty.

'Any problems?' asked Sophie.

'No. She came round quickly and easily and she's gone back to sleep now.'

'Right, thank you. Come on, Jefferson, let's take her back to her mum and to a nice warm bed,' said Sophie. Together they transferred the little girl to the trolley.

'Wait a minute,' said the staff nurse, as they made to leave the recovery room. 'Won't you be wanting this?'

As Sophie turned she saw the other nurse was holding up Rosie, whom someone had wrapped in Chloe's piece of patchwork.

'Heavens, yes.' Taking the doll and the material, Sophie tucked them in beside the sleeping child. 'We'd be in all sorts of trouble if she woke up without those.'

A short while later they were back in the ward and had transferred Chloe to her bed. Mrs Stewart was hovering anxiously throughout the procedure. 'Is she all right?' she asked at last.

'She's fine,' Sophie replied. 'She came round for a little while but she's gone back to sleep again. I have to check her blood pressure, so maybe you'd like to sit beside her and hold her other hand. That way, when she wakes she'll see you first. But before that maybe you would like to put a dressing pad on Rosie's tummy.'

Sophie kept up her regular post-op observations on Chloe, who remained very sleepy
for a couple of hours. When she finally woke
up, she was rather distressed with pain and had
to be given an analgesic.

Towards the end of her shift Sophie attended a staff meeting in Sister's office, where
the ward staff were briefed on the coming admission of Antonia Brett, and when it was over
she made her way to the staff canteen for a
quick snack.

She had no sooner settled herself at a table
with a sandwich and her usual glass of orange
juice, and was thinking over what Sister had
just told her, when a voice broke into her
thoughts.

'May I join you?'

Her heart leapt as she recognised his voice
and it was barely necessary to even look up to
confirm the fact. Benedict was standing before
her. He'd changed out of his theatre greens and
was wearing his white coat once more. It was
unbuttoned, as usual, his stethoscope was protruding from his top pocket, as usual, and, as
usual, the dark hair was tousled. And if all that

wasn't enough, to complete the air of utter familiarity, that look of amusement was also right there in those fascinating green-flecked eyes of his.

CHAPTER FOUR

'OF COURSE.' Sophie moved her tray to enable Benedict to set down his own lunch on the table.

'Actually,' he said as he slid into the seat, 'you're just the person I wanted to see.'

'Oh?' Sophie found she couldn't meet his gaze.

'Yes. I wanted to ask you about Antonia Brett.'

'Antonia?' She did look up then, surprised by what he'd said. For a moment she'd imagined the reason he wanted to see her had something to do with the apartment.

'Yes.' He nodded. 'Everyone seems to know her and to know everything about her. I wondered if you could fill me in before I look up her notes. You know what I mean—her personal history, that sort of thing.'

'Of course.' She paused. 'Do you know *any-thing* about her?'

'Well, I gather she's a cancer patient?'

'Yes, she is,' Sophie agreed. 'Antonia first came to us about two years ago when she was only nine years old. She'd been experiencing tiredness, nausea and pain in her abdomen. She underwent many tests and eventually was diagnosed with a malignant growth in her abdomen.'

'Was she with Mr Crowley-Smith?'

'She was, and she underwent extensive surgery, followed by chemotherapy. Eventually, after a long stay with us she was able to go home, although she returned on a regular basis for outpatient appointments.'

Sophie smiled reflectively. 'On those occasions she always came up to the ward to see us. After a time she was even well enough to return to school. Since her tenth birthday, however, she's had a year of ups and downs. Sometimes, apparently, she seemed quite well, at other times she would feel tired and nauseous and have to stay in bed. More investigations followed and it was decided that there was no further treatment that could be given and that Antonia's illness was terminal.'

'Ah,' said Benedict softly, 'that explains people's reactions to the fact that she's being admitted again.'

'It was only a matter of time, and I suppose subconsciously it was something we'd all been waiting for. As you will have gathered, we've all become very fond of Antonia and, for that matter, of her family as well.'

'I can imagine.' Benedict nodded. He was silent for a moment, as if reflecting on what Sophie had just told him, then he spoke again. 'Tell me about her family,' he said. 'No doubt I shall be having quite extensive dealings with them in the weeks to come.'

'They're a very close family,' Sophie replied. 'There are her parents, Jill and Mike, her older brother, Sean, and younger sister, Fleur. They've all been very involved with Antonia's illness from the very beginning.'

'And are they all aware of the prognosis?'

'I think by now, yes, probably they are—but much care and counselling will be required for them all.'

'Absolutely.' Benedict nodded. 'Well, thanks for putting me in the picture. I can see why everyone seems so bound up with

Antonia, yet at the same time I sensed a certain reluctance to talk about her. It was difficult to know how to approach the situation.' He paused and took a mouthful of his coffee. 'Now, the other thing I wanted to ask you was whether or not you'd thought any more about the apartment.'

'Oh, yes,' Sophie replied with a laugh. 'In fact, I'd go so far as to say I've thought of little else.'

'Really?' He raised his eyebrows in apparent surprise. 'But have you done anything about it?'

'Well, I collected the details from the agent on the way home last night. I then discussed it with my parents who, I might add, thought that it sounded like a very good proposition, so at nine o'clock this morning I rang the agent and said I was interested.'

'And?' Benedict's air of surprise was replaced by one of amusement at her apparent enthusiasm.

'They've arranged a viewing for me for later today. I'm meeting someone there at four o'clock.'

'Well, that's marvellous. So this means in a very short space of time you and I could be neighbours.'

'Yes,' she said with a smile. 'I suppose it does.'

They fell silent, but as the silence grew uncomfortable Sophie found she was desperately searching for something to say. If anyone had asked her to say why it was uncomfortable she would have been at a loss to explain, but she knew it had something to do with the prospect of living in such close proximity to this man who had stirred her emotions since the moment she'd set eyes upon him. At last, and changing the subject, she said, 'Have you got your car back yet?'

He shook his head. 'No. I've just phoned the garage. It was supposed to have been ready today, but they had to send away for a part and it hasn't arrived yet. Mine is no ordinary car, you see—it's really very elderly and it needs lots of tender loving care.'

'I see.' Sophie laughed. 'Well, in that case, I guess you'll be wanting a lift down to the town again.'

'That's kind of you. I'll go indoors and get the kettle on. I'm sure you'll be glad of a cuppa when you've had a tour of your new apartment.'

Somehow she couldn't refuse. How could she when he was simply being so kind? And, besides, what harm could there be in two pro-spective neighbours having a friendly cup of tea together?

Antonia Brett looked tired and very, very pale when she arrived on the ward in a wheelchair pushed by her father, Mike, but her smile was as bright and sparkling as it had always been.

'Hello, Antonia,' said Sophie with, she hoped, an equally beaming smile. It was hard to remain cheerful because her breath had caught in her throat when she'd seen the little girl and had realised just how much she'd de-teriorated since her last visit to the ward.

'Hi, Nurse Sophie. I hope you've got my favourite corner ready for me,' said Antonia as she looked up at Sophie from beneath the brim of her black velvet hat.

'We certainly have—corner bed by the win-dow. That's right, isn't it?' When Antonia grinned and nodded, Sophie added, 'All you have to do is put up your Boyzone posters.'

'I'll do that for her,' said the tall, good-looking young boy by her side.

'Good heavens!' Sophie exclaimed. 'It's Sean. Honestly, you've grown so much I hardly recognised you.'

'I've hardly grown at all,' said the small girl on the other side of the wheelchair.

'Hello, Fleur,' said Sophie. 'I shouldn't worry about being small. My grandmother always used to say that the best things come in small parcels.'

'I hope we're not too early.' Jill Brett, Antonia's mother, stepped forward, carrying her daughter's belongings in a holdall. 'The thing is, it's Sean's and Fleur's lunch-hour from school and they were adamant they wanted to come in with Antonia.'

'Of course. After all, this is a family affair,' Sophie replied briskly, only too aware of the heartbreak that was underlying the family's brave front.

She left them to it for a while, after accompanying them to Antonia's corner. They were well used to the procedures, having gone through them so many times before.

Andrea was at the nurses' station and on meeting Sophie's gaze she raised her eyebrows, her silence adequately expressing what they were all thinking since catching sight of Antonia.

In the end it was Sophie herself who put it into words. 'I knew it had to be bad,' she murmured, 'for her to be coming back here, but I have to admit I didn't expect her to be looking quite like this.'

'Poor little mite,' said Andrea. 'Let's hope we can make things as happy as possible while she's here.'

When Sophie returned to the cubicle in the corner it was to find that Mike had lifted his daughter from her wheelchair onto her bed, where she was lying propped up against her pillows, still fully dressed.

'She's exhausted,' said Jill to Sophie. 'The journey has really taken it out of her.'

'We'll pop her into bed when she's had a bit of a rest,' Sophie replied. 'Are you staying?' she added.

Jill nodded. 'Yes. We've worked out shifts so that at least, for most of the time, one of us will be here with Antonia. I shall be here for the rest of the afternoon. Mike and the children will come back for the evening, then I shall be here again for the night.'

'That's great,' said Sophie. 'Now, if we can just complete the admission forms—you must know them by heart by now.'

'Is a doctor coming to see Antonia?' asked Mike as he and his son finished putting Antonia's favourite posters around her bed.

'Mr Crowley-Smith will be along to see her in the morning,' said Sophie. 'But we just want Antonia to rest for the time being.'

As she finished speaking Antonia lifted her head. 'Will Dr Evans be coming in the morning as well?' she said.

'Dr Evans isn't here any more,' Sophie replied. 'We have a new registrar—his name is Dr Lawrence.'

'Is he nice?' asked Antonia.

'Oh, yes,' said Sophie. 'He is. He's very nice. I'm sure you'll like him.'

'I think we'll get going now,' said Mike with a glance at his watch, 'and leave Nurse

Sophie to get on with her forms.' He leaned over the bed to kiss his daughter. 'Bye-bye, pumpkin,' he said. 'Be good. We'll be back later to see you.'

After the departure of the rest of the Brett family, Sophie completed Antonia's admission forms. Then with Jill's help she assisted Antonia into bed. Leaving the girl to rest, she drew the curtains around the cubicle and moved away down the ward.

As Sophie passed Chloe's bed she paused and looked at the little girl who was fully awake now. 'Hello,' she said. 'How are you feeling?'

'All right,' whispered Chloe, while her mother glanced up from the magazine she was reading and smiled.

'She seems much better since she had the medicine,' she said.

'Rosie's better, too,' said Chloe. 'She had medicine as well.'

'Well, I'm glad about that,' Sophie replied with a smile. 'I'm going off duty now, but I'll see you in the morning.'

'Bye, Nurse Sophie...' said Chloe sleepily.

*   *   *

Benedict was waiting for her in the car park. It was another cold day but, instead of the chill winds of the day before, today's was a crisp cold following a sharp, early morning frost.

'Do you think we could be expecting a white Christmas?' he said as he got into the car and began blowing in his cupped hands in an attempt to warm them.

'I doubt it,' said Sophie as she tried to clear her windscreen. 'I can't remember the last time it snowed this far south at Christmas, although I must admit the idea is a lovely one.'

'I can remember several Christmases where it snowed back home in Norfolk,' he said. Then he paused, as if reflecting, and as Sophie drew out of the car park he went on, 'There was one particular Christmas when we sang carols around the front door of the local manor house while the snow gently fell onto our shoulders, and afterwards the squire and his lady asked us inside for mulled wine and hot mince pies. There was a huge Christmas tree in the hall, lit with thousands of white lights, and the rafters were decked with boughs of holly and mistletoe. I would love another Christmas like that.'

Sophie threw him a sideways glance. 'It sounds to me, Dr Lawrence,' she said, 'as if you're an incurable romantic.'

'Oh, I am,' he said seriously. 'Believe me, I am.'

The estate agent was waiting for them at Clifton Court and Benedict accompanied him and Sophie up to the second floor where the agent unlocked the empty apartment.

As he stood aside for her to enter the flat, Sophie, on a sudden impulse, turned to Benedict. 'You come in as well,' she said.

Without a word he followed them inside. Once over the threshold Sophie paused to look around, and as she did so she was suddenly swamped by a feeling of certainty, a feeling that told her that this place was right and, thanks to her grandmother's legacy, could be home.

It was similar in layout to Benedict's flat but the decor was different, being in soft autumnal tones and with its main windows overlooking the internal courtyard that housed a small fountain. The bathroom was tiled in dusky pink and the kitchen theme was terracotta and turquoise.

As Sophie moved from room to room she was filled with a growing sense of excitement.

'I love it,' she said at last. 'It's just what I'm looking for.'

After the estate agent had gone, with a promise to Sophie that the appropriate forms would be in the post the following day, Benedict turned to her. 'Time for that cup of tea?' he asked.

'Oh, yes,' she replied happily. 'Yes, I think so.'

'Come on, I'll put the kettle on. I feel really it should be champagne, but I don't have any so we'll have to wait till another time for that.' He unlocked his apartment and led the way inside.

'I can't believe it has all been so simple,' said Sophie, watching him as he filled the kettle then lifted teapot and mugs from one of the kitchen cupboards. 'And, really, it's thanks to you. If you hadn't mentioned this flat coming back on the market it would have been snapped up and I wouldn't have known anything about it.'

'I guess some things are just meant to be.' He turned from the cupboard and his gaze met hers. Once again Sophie found herself quickly looking away, totally unable to cope with what she saw in his eyes.

When he had brewed the tea he carried the tray from the kitchen into his sitting-room, where they sat opposite each other in the deep, leather sofas on either side of a glass-topped coffee-table.

'So how soon will you be able to move in?' he asked as he passed her a mug of tea.

'As soon as everything is finalised, I should think. It usually takes a couple of weeks for all the legalities to go through.'

'All being well, then, you should be in for Christmas.'

'That would be marvellous—although, like you, I've actually volunteered to work on Christmas Day.' She took a sip of tea. 'Talking of work, Antonia Brett arrived on the ward just after I was talking to you.'

'Really?' He looked up in surprise. 'I thought she wasn't due until this afternoon.'

'She wasn't, but her brother and sister came with her in their school dinner-hour.'

'That's nice—they sound a really supportive family.'

'Oh, they are,' Sophie agreed. 'There's absolutely no doubt about that.'

'How was she? Antonia, I mean.'

'She looked very frail. In fact, far worse than any of us were expecting. I'm afraid it's very obvious that her illness is now terminal.'

'Like you said, she's going to need lots of tender loving care.'

Sophie nodded. 'She asked if Dr Evans would be in to see her and I told her he was no longer with us, but I went on to tell her that you were our new registrar.'

'I must go and see her in the morning,' Benedict replied. 'I'll need to spend a bit of time with her and get to know her.'

'She'll appreciate that. She's a lovely child. Life seems so unfair sometimes.'

They sat on, drinking their tea and discussing the hospital, until at last Sophie glanced at her watch. 'Heavens,' she said. 'Is that the time? I really must be going. Thank you so much, Benedict, for all your kindness.' She rose to her feet, somewhat reluctantly, aware of the fact that she could quite happily have sat there chatting to him for ever as the dusk descended around them at the end of the short winter's afternoon.

'Not at all...' He, too, stood up and she sensed the same reluctance in him that this time together should be brought to a close. 'Do you have to go?' he asked, confirming her suspicions.

'I'm sorry...?' She looked at him quickly.

'What I meant was...couldn't you stay awhile...maybe have something to eat...?'

At that precise moment there was nothing in the world she would have liked better than to stay there with him while he prepared a meal, then to share it with him while they continued to talk, to get to know each other, but somewhere at the back of her mind there niggled that little voice of reason.

'No,' she said at last. 'No, really. It is very kind of you but I really do have to go. My mother will be expecting me...'

What she didn't say and probably what she should have said was that because of her relationship with Miles she really shouldn't be sitting in another man's apartment, leading him to believe that she was free and available. But somehow she found she couldn't mention

Miles. She had the feeling that soon she might have to tell Benedict about him, but not yet, not today.

The lights glittered in the tinsel-bedecked shop windows as Sophie drove across town, and a Salvation Army band was playing carols around the huge Christmas tree in the square. She smiled as she wound down the window, caught a few bars of 'While Shepherds Watched Their Flocks by Night' and thought of Benedict and his story about his romantic Christmases past in Norfolk. Briefly she wondered about his home and who he still had in Norfolk, and as she reached her own family home she resolved she would ask him about it the next opportunity she had.

He'd sounded wistful when he'd spoken of the past. Maybe he was lonely and missing his family. The least she could do was give him the opportunity to talk about them, especially at this time of goodwill, this time which was supposedly to be spent with families and loved ones—that is, if you don't work for the health service, she thought drily as she parked her car.

Her mother was out and Sophie found a note to say she'd gone to her bridge afternoon with the ladies of the club she belonged to. She felt a slight sense of disappointment—she'd been looking forward to telling her mother about the apartment. Her father was obviously still in surgery so she couldn't tell him. Suddenly she felt she simply had to tell someone and on an impulse she decided to ring the number of Miles's mobile phone and give him the good news. He had given her the mobile number as, he'd said, the ringing of the house phone always seemed to disturb his father.

He didn't answer until the twelfth ring when Sophie had been on the point of hanging up.

'Hello,' he said when he'd heard her voice, 'This is a surprise—two days running.'

'I didn't think you were able to answer.'

'I'd left my phone in my jacket pocket in the bedroom. I only heard it ringing by chance.'

'What's all that noise I can hear?' she asked with a laugh.

'It's children playing outside in the next-door garden. I'll just shut the window. That's better. Goodness knows what they're doing out there in the dark—they're kicking up the most unholy racket. Dad's getting really agitated about it. I guess I'll have to go and sort them out if it doesn't stop soon. Anyway, how are you, my love?' His voice softened. 'This is a nice surprise. I really wasn't expecting to speak to you again today.'

'I know. But I had to ring, Miles. I wanted to tell you. I went to see the flat. It was lovely and I more or less made up my mind on the spot that I'm going to have it.'

'Well, that's great.' He paused. 'When do you think you'll be able to move in?'

'Probably in a couple of weeks or so.'

'So do you think you'll be in by the time I come down?'

'Hopefully, yes…' She paused, for some reason uneasy at that thought.

'It sounds like you and I are going to have to have our own pre-Christmas celebration, doesn't it?'

'Yes…yes, it does.' Mention of the word 'celebration' had suddenly conjured up a picture of Benedict when he'd mentioned not having any champagne to celebrate her decision to buy the flat but that it could be remedied later.

'Is there anything wrong?' asked Miles.

'No. Why?'

'You suddenly sounded rather distant.'

'Really? No, I'm fine... A bit tired, I suppose, but, then, I usually am after a long shift.'

'So how's work?'

'It's OK. You know, the usual.'

'Old Crowley-Smith as much of a stuffed shirt as ever?'

'Oh, he's not that bad.' She paused. 'I keep forgetting you knew him.'

'Hardly that. I doubt he even knew I existed in those days. He was at the General in Manchester for years. I could never figure out how he kept any of his staff. I always thought he seemed an impossible man. Or maybe he only saved that obnoxious manner for medical reps.'

'I think he's probably mellowed a bit since those days,' Sophie replied. 'And he's very highly thought of, you know. He has a new registrar at the moment—a Dr Lawrence. He applied for the job here purely so that he could work with him.'

'Well, rather him than me.' Miles replied with an audible grunt. 'Anyway,' he went on in a lighter tone, 'that's enough of all this shop talk. How about you telling me how much you miss me?'

'You know I do, Miles,' protested Sophie.

'And I miss you, too, my love. I just wish there weren't all these obstacles to us being together. Let's hope it won't be for too much longer, then I can prove it to you.'

After they'd said goodnight and Sophie had hung up, she found herself going back over what they'd said and wondering quite how the new registrar's name had come up. She certainly hadn't intended to say anything about Benedict, but it seemed he'd just come quite naturally into the conversation. And really, she thought, that was just as it was when also, quite naturally, she found herself thinking about him at the very oddest of moments.

CHAPTER FIVE

'YOU'VE done what?' Andrea stared at her in astonishment.

'I've bought an apartment,' Sophie repeated patiently.

'Where? How?' Andrea looked bewildered.

'I recently received a legacy from my grand-mother,' Sophie replied, taking Andrea's second question first. It was the morning after her conversation with Miles and the two girls were sharing a coffee-break in the staffroom.

'Lucky old you. When did all this happen? You haven't said anything about it before.'

'Well, my gran died last year, as you know, and I knew my brother and I were her chief beneficiaries but I didn't know exactly how much I'd inherited until her estate was wound up. I hadn't really thought about buying property but what with the lease on my other flat expiring, then this apartment coming up, and my dad saying it would be a good invest-ment...'

'So where is it?' Andrea sounded excited now.

Sophie took a deep breath and, setting her mug down on the table in front of her, she said, 'It's one of those new ones on the old brewery site.'

'Oh.' Andrea stared at her then, as the penny dropped, she said, 'But isn't that where you said Benedict Lawrence has a place?'

'Yes, it is.' Sophie nodded, trying to appear casual but, she feared, failing miserably, which was ridiculous really because there was no reason on earth why she should feel uncomfortable just because she was buying an apartment in the same block as the new paediatric registrar.

'How did all this come about?' Andrea was frowning now.

'Well, you know I gave him a lift home the other night?'

'Yes?' Her friend was looking faintly incredulous now, as if she knew she wasn't going to be able to quite believe what she was about to hear.

'When we got to the apartments he told me that there was one on which the sale had fallen through and that it was about to go back on the market. I suppose I showed my interest because he invited me inside—'

'What, to see this apartment?'

'Er, no, not exactly… It was locked, but he did show me around his own apartment, which he said was very similar to the empty one. Just so that I could get the feel of the place and see if I liked it,' she added, when Andrea continued to stare at her.

'And did you?' asked Andrea at last.

'Did I what?'

'Like it?'

'Oh, yes, it was very nice.'

'I bet it was,' said Andrea drily. 'So did you decide there and then? On the spot, so to speak?'

'Yes, I suppose I did really. I called into the estate agency on the way home to get the rest of the details, then I discussed it with my parents and slept on it, before finally making a decision.'

'And what about Miles—did you discuss it with him, too?'

Sophie nodded. 'Yes, I did.'

'And what did he say?'

'Well, I think he was pleased about the fact that I would be having my own place again—it hasn't been easy on the last few occasions when he's been down, me being at my parents'.'

'But…?'

'But what?' Sophie glanced up sharply.

'I thought there was a but coming there. You said Miles was pleased that you would be in your own place again, then you stopped.'

'Did I? Well, I suppose what I was going to say was that he seemed a bit put out because he'd thought that we might have been buying a place together.'

'So why aren't you?' Andrea raised her eyebrows.

'The time isn't right.' Sophie frowned. 'Miles really can't leave his father at the present time…but there will be a right time and, in the meantime, this place will be a jolly good investment.'

'You can say that again,' said Andrea with a short laugh.

'What do you mean?'

'Well, I was just visualising those cosy dinner parties that you'll be able to have in the future.'

'I'm not with you.' Sophie shook her head, wondering just what her friend was getting at.

'Well, you and Miles, and me and Benedict Lawrence, of course.' Andrea laughed again, drained her mug, then stood up. 'Come on, it's time we got back. Old Bill Bailey will be doing her nut.'

Slowly Sophie followed her friend out of the staffroom, wondering why the picture Andrea had just painted of a cosy foursome had so disturbed her.

When they got back to the ward it was to find that Sister Bailey was indeed in a bit of a flap because during the time the two staff nurses had been gone for their coffee-break the doctors had decided to arrive for their morning ward round. 'And as if that wasn't enough,' snapped Sister Bailey, 'when the round was over and they'd gone, Dr Lawrence came back.'

'Came back?' Andrea looked round the ward with interest. 'Where is he?'

'He's talking to Antonia and her mother,' Sister Bailey replied. 'Right,' she went on briskly, 'now that you're back, Andrea, I want you to do an admission, and, Sophie, I want you to change Chloe's dressing.'

Sophie was glad to be doing something away from Andrea's scrutiny. Pobably for the first time since she and Andrea had become friends she found herself uncomfortable in the other girl's presence, and she wasn't really sure why. It was nothing tangible, nothing she was really able to put her finger on, but there was something there between them now like an invisible barrier.

She puzzled over it while she set up the dressing trolley in the treatment room, but she was no closer to finding the answer when she emerged into the ward ten minutes later, pushing the trolley before her. As she reached Chloe's bed she heard peals of laughter coming from the corner of the ward. Glancing across to Antonia's corner, she saw Benedict perched on the edge of the bed while Antonia and her mother were laughing uproariously at something he'd said. Their laughter was infectious and Sophie couldn't prevent a smile herself as she manoeuvered her trolley alongside Chloe's bed.

Mrs Stewart had just finished washing her daughter's face and she looked up and smiled at Sophie. 'Someone sounds happy,' she said. 'It's lovely to hear that little girl laugh.'

'Dr Ben has been telling her jokes,' said Chloe solemnly. 'He told me one yesterday. It was funny but I can't 'member it now.'

'Don't worry, Chloe,' said Sophie with a sigh. 'I can't remember jokes either, and if I do I forget the punchline. Now, Chloe, I want to have a look at your tummy, please.'

'What about Rosie's?' asked Chloe as she wriggled down in the bed and Sophie drew the curtains.

'Oh, yes, Rosie's as well, of course.' Carefully Sophie rolled up Chloe's nightgown, revealing the white gauze pad on her abdomen.

Propping herself up on her elbows, Chloe peered down at the site of her wound. 'Oh,' she gasped as she caught sight of two small spots of blood which had leaked through the dressing. 'It's been bleeding!'

'It's all right, Chloe.' Sophie hastened to reassure her. 'It's only a little bit and it's dried, which means it happened some time ago, so it isn't bleeding now. What I'm going to do is to lift this dressing pad off and put on a nice, clean, fresh one.'

'Will it hurt?' The little girl's eyes were like saucers.

'Not at all. I'm the best dressing taker-off on the ward,' Sophie replied. 'But what I'd like you to do while I'm doing it, if you would, is to change Rosie's dressing.' She glanced across the bed at Mrs Stewart, who picked up Rosie and passed her to her daughter. Chloe dutifully lifted the rag doll's green, knitted dress, revealing her dressing patch, and while she proceeded to peel off the strips of tape securing the pad, in the blink of an eye, Sophie removed the little girl's own dressing.

'May I come in?' The curtains around the bed parted about an inch and someone peered through.

'It's Dr Ben!' squealed Chloe.

He opened the curtains wider and eased himself inside. 'Hi, Chloe, how's Rosie?' he asked, leaning over to inspect the rag doll.

'She's better—look,' replied Chloe solemnly.

'Well, that's very good, I must say,' Benedict replied. 'And what about you?' He looked down at Chloe's wound. 'Nice and healthy, I would say, Nurse Sophie. Wouldn't you?'

His gaze met Sophie's and she saw the suppressed merriment there. 'Absolutely, Dr Ben,' she agreed.

'Does it still hurt, Chloe?' He looked down at the little girl again.

'Yes.' She nodded. 'When I sit up it does.'

'How are the obs?' He glanced at Sophie again.

'Temperature is still up a little and pulse was rapid early this morning.'

'I think a little more paracetamol today,' he said. 'I'll write her up for some. Then, if all is well tomorrow, we can start talking about going home.' He smiled at Mrs Stewart as he said this, and with a wink at Chloe he moved out of the cubicle, leaving Sophie to put clean dressing pads on both Chloe and Rosie. When she'd finished she began clearing the empty dressing packs.

'Sam is coming to see me today, isn't he, Mummy?' said Chloe anxiously.

'Yes, darling, he'll be along with Daddy after school.'

'I'll leave you to it for a while,' said Sophie as she drew back the curtains and wheeled the trolley out into the gangway. 'Later we'll get Chloe out of bed and take her for a little walk.'

As Sophie moved off down the ward she heard Chloe say, 'Mummy, what's a punchline?'

Sophie was still smiling when she got back to the treatment room, where she found Benedict talking to Mollie and Andrea. While she busied herself with disposing of the rubbish from her trolley, before cleaning and disinfecting the trolley itself, Sophie realised that the others were discussing a child who'd just been sent up to the ward from the accident and emergency unit.

'As far as I can make out, he's severely traumatised,' said Andrea.

'Has Sister sent for the clinical psychologist?' asked Benedict.

'Yes, that's Rosemary Lennard—she's on her way up, apparently,' Andrea replied. 'I understand the police are involved as well.'

Sophie turned from the sink in concern at what she was hearing. 'Whatever has happened?' she asked.

'It seems there was some sort of fight or attack at the boy's home.' It was Benedict who replied. 'He's been injured and his mother and sister are in Intensive Care.'

'How old is he?' asked Sophie.

'Seven, I think,' Andrea replied. Turning to Mollie, she added, 'That's right, isn't it, Mollie?'

The care worker nodded. 'Yes, poor little love. I wish I could get my hands on the person responsible. His little sister is only three, apparently. Someone down in Cas said it was touch and go where the mother was concerned.' The fury in her voice was only too evident, and as Sophie felt her own anger surge she looked at Benedict and saw her own emotion reflected in his eyes.

'Who's with him now?' she asked, looking at Andrea.

'Sister and Dr Hewlett, but I must get back. Someone is going to have to sit with him all the time, even though he's been sedated.'

The others dispersed, and when Sophie herself had finished in the treatment room she emerged to find the rest of the ward, staff and patients alike, strangely subdued, the laughter of earlier somehow forgotten now in the face of this new life-and-death drama being played out in their midst.

Hazel Bailey held a staff case conference later in the day concerning the child who had been admitted to the ward from the accident and emergency unit. Benedict attended, representing both himself and Franklin Crowley-Smith, who was in Theatre. The paediatric clinical psychologist, Rosemary Lennard, was also present, as were the duty social worker, the liaison health visitor, Bianca Phelps, and several members of the paediatric ward staff. At the last moment Sister Bailey asked Sophie to attend. Andrea was still sitting with the child.

Somehow they all managed to squeeze into Sister's office, and after she'd given a preliminary briefing Sister Bailey invited social worker Lindsey Wright to fill in as many of the details as she could.

Lindsey collected up a sheaf of papers, setting them in a neat pile before her on Sister's desk. 'This is a particularly disturbing case,' she said, looking round the room at the ring of grim, silent faces, 'and especially difficult because neither we at Social Services nor the police had had any previous dealings with the family. The children weren't known to us, neither were they on an at-risk register.'

'Do the police have any idea what happened to them?' asked Samir, the young Romanian houseman, his dark eyes filled with concern.

Linsey nodded. 'Yes, although at this point it is, of course, only conjecture. We think, early this morning, the children's mother opened the front door of her home to someone. This person, whoever it was, was either invited into the house or forced his way in. The police are of the opinion that it was someone known to the children's mother and that she actually let him in because there was no sign of a struggle in the hallway.'

'So where did the attack take place?' asked Benedict. He was standing with his back to the door, his arms folded. There was now in his eyes no trace of the amusement that had been there earlier.

'Upstairs,' Lindsey replied quietly. 'We believe, in the mother's bedroom—at least that was where the little girl was found. The mother was on the landing—the police think she managed to crawl out there before she collapsed. As you probably know, both the mother and the little girl are in Intensive Care. The mother has a fractured skull and the child is having difficulties with her breathing, following, we think, a blow to her windpipe. The mother had also been sexually assaulted.'

'And the boy?' said Benedict, as everyone in the room seemed to hold his or her breath.

'It was Tom who raised the alarm,' Lindsey replied. 'Although badly injured himself, he got to the phone and dialled 999.'

'Where is the children's father?' asked a tight-lipped Sister Bailey.

'He lives in Hull. He and the mother are divorced. Apparently he's on his way down.'

'Is he to be allowed in to see Tom?' asked Sophie.

'Yes.' Lindsey nodded. 'A police officer will be on duty here so any visitors will be carefully monitored. 'We are awaiting background reports on the family from their GP and their health visitor, who would still be visiting them in respect of the little girl. We have also contacted Tom's primary school to see if they can shed any light on the family circumstances.' She glanced up. 'Right, Sister,' she concluded, 'thank you very much—it's over to you.'

Sister Bailey nodded. 'Thank you. I don't need to tell you,' she said, glancing round at the members of her team, 'that this child is going to need lots of care and patience if he is to recover from his dreadful ordeal. Isn't that right, Rosemary?' She turned to the psychologist who nodded in agreement.

'With regard to his injuries…' She paused and consulted a piece of paper on the desk before her. 'He suffered a severe beating and has injuries to his head and face. There is extensive bruising around his left eye, his right arm is broken and there are lacerations to his body and legs, as well as much further bruising. X-rays were taken in A and E and show two cracked ribs and damage to one kidney.'

She paused for a long moment then, taking a deep breath, she went on, 'I feel, however, that while we can cope with his injuries and heal them, the psychological damage may take much longer.' Those around her nodded their agreement. 'Well, thank you all for attending,' she concluded.

They filed out of the office in silence, all deeply affected by what they had just heard. Sophie made her way back onto the ward, where Antonia's mother beckoned to her.

'What is it?' As she approached the bed in the corner Sophie could see that the curtains were drawn around it and from within came the unmistakable sound of sobbing.

'She's terribly upset,' whispered Jill Brett.

'Do you know what's wrong?' Sophie had a sudden premonition that the realization that she was going to die had finally hit Antonia.

'Not really,' Jill whispered back. 'She'd been very quiet for a couple of hours or so then this crying started and I can't really get anything out of her.'

'Why don't you leave her with me for a little while?' said Sophie softly. 'Go and have a coffee and a breath of fresh air.'

'Well…' Jill hesitated, glancing uncertainly at the drawn curtains.

'Go on,' said Sophie. 'You deserve a break. I'll try and have a chat with her.'

'All right, then,' said Jill rather reluctantly with another worried, lingering glance towards her daughter's bed. 'But I'll only be in the rest room if she wants me.'

As Jill disappeared down the ward Sophie opened the curtains a little and slipped inside the cubicle. Antonia was lying on her bed with her face turned to the wall as she sobbed into a soggy tissue. The black velvet hat that she usually wore was lying beside her on the pillow, revealing her wispy fair hair which had just started to grow again after all the chemotherapy she'd had.

'Antonia,' said Sophie softly, closing the curtains behind her, 'what is it? Can you tell me about it?'

The child stopped sobbing for a moment and turned her tear-stained face towards Sophie to see who had come into her cubicle. When she saw it was Sophie she began to sob all the more.

Steeling herself to face questions about death and the nature of dying, Sophie sat on the edge of the bed and gathered Antonia into her arms, allowing the young girl to work through the storm of her weeping while Sophie gently stroked the soft down on her head.

At last the girl's sobs began to subside until they were little more than a series of shuddering hiccups.

'It sometimes helps, you know, if you can talk about it,' said Sophie at last. 'And sometimes it's difficult to talk about these things to those closest to you. Tell me, Antonia, are you worrying about your illness? Are you frightened?'

Antonia shook her head. 'No,' she said. 'No, it's not that. You see, I know I'm going to die. Sometimes people think I don't know that. But I do and I'm not afraid, Sophie. I'm really not.'

Sophie swallowed. 'I believe you, Antonia,' she said at last. Her voice came out strange, sort of squeaky and husky, not like her voice at all. 'So if it isn't that you're upset about…?'

'It's that little boy,' whispered Antonia. 'The one they brought in earlier.'

Sophie caught her breath. 'Yes?' she said. 'You mean Tom?'

'Is that his name? I didn't know.' Antonia's eyes had grown wide with anger and fear. 'I saw him. And I heard him. He was crying. I had gone to the loo and I saw Jefferson and another porter bring him into the ward. He was all covered up with sheets and bandages. I thought he must have been run over by a car...but then...I heard...I heard...' By this time her eyes were brimming with tears again.

'Yes,' prompted Sophie. 'What did you hear?'

As the tears spilled over and trickled slowly down her cheeks, Antonia gulped. 'I heard Jefferson and the other man talking.'

Sophie stiffened and Antonia threw her a quick glance. 'It wasn't their fault,' she said. 'They didn't know I was there. I was behind the bathroom door. I wasn't hiding—I just stood there out of the way so that they could get past with the trolley.'

'All right.' Sophie nodded. 'So what exactly did you hear?'

'They said he...the little boy had been beaten up. They said his mother and his little sister had been attacked as well and that they'd nearly died. Then Jefferson said if he could catch…the…the bastard who'd done it he would string him up by—'

'Yes, all right, Antonia,' Sophie hastily interrupted. 'But you mustn't get so upset, you know. Tom is safe now. We're caring for him.'

'Yes, I know.' Antonia gave another shuddering hiccup that seemed to rack her frail, emaciated little body. 'But I couldn't stop thinking about him and about what had happened to him. Then I tried to imagine how I would have felt if it was Sean and Fleur and my mummy that it had happened to…'

'Oh, Antonia.' With a deep sigh Sophie drew the little girl into her arms again and hugged her close. For a moment she was completely overwhelmed by the child's generosity of spirit in the face of her own appalling problems.

'He will be all right, won't he?' said Antonia at last, breaking the silence.

'Yes, he will,' Sophie replied. 'And there's a good chance that his mother and his sister will make a full recovery as well. But listen, I tell you what, why don't you and I go down to where Tom is, then you can see him for yourself?'

'Could I really do that?' Antonia looked up in surprise.

'I don't see why not,' Sophie replied. 'Come on, let's slip your dressing-gown on. That's right—now your slippers.' Antonia swung her legs to the floor and thrust her feet into a pair of rabbit's-head slippers. Drawing back the curtains, they stepped out into the ward and began the short walk to the other end where Tom was in one of the small side rooms reserved for children who were either very ill or who required special nursing.

Outside in the corridor Sophie could see a uniformed policeman guarding the entrance to the ward, but she decided not to mention that fact to Antonia. Instead, she peered through the glass partition into the side room where she could see that both Benedict and Andrea were in attendance on the boy. Lightly she tapped on the glass and they both looked up. Opening the door, she said, 'How is he?' At the same time she glanced at the little figure in the bed, swathed in bandages.

'He's come round,' said Benedict. 'The sed-atives are wearing off but he's still rather woozy.'

'I've brought Antonia to see him,' Sophie began.

'Antonia?' Andrea looked startled and even Benedict looked up in surprise.

'Antonia has been very worried about Tom,' explained Sophie. 'Apparently she overheard certain things when he came in and it upset her, just thinking about him. I thought it might be a good idea to bring her down so that she can see him for herself.' With that she stood aside so that Benedict and Andrea could see the little figure with the wispy hair, standing forlornly in the doorway in her pink fluffy dressing-gown and her rabbit slippers.

'Well, of course,' exclaimed Benedict. 'What a good idea. Hello, Antonia. Come on in, poppet.'

Slowly Antonia approached the bed, watched by the three members of staff. Tom was lying half on his side, propped up by pil-lows. He had a bandage round his head which also covered one eye. The other eye was swol-len and almost closed, one arm was in plaster and there was a tube inserted into one of his nostrils and another in a cannula in his left hand which was attached to a saline drip.

'Hello, Tom. My name is Antonia.' Bending down so that Tom could see her through the one half-open eye, she added, 'I wanted to see if you were feeling any better.'

There wasn't as much as a flicker from the still little form on the bed but, undaunted, Antonia reached out and touched his good hand, which lay motionless on the white cellular blanket that covered him. 'I'm in a bed outside in the ward,' she went on. 'I shall come and see you every day.'

With the barest of movements the little boy's mouth stretched into what could have been the semblance of a smile, and with a little sigh of satisfaction Antonia straightened up. As she did so she swayed slightly, and Benedict moved swiftly forward and scooped her up into his arms.

'I think, young lady,' he said, 'you've quite worn yourself out. Come on, it's back to bed for you. Like you said, you can come and see Tom again tomorrow.'

With that he carried Antonia out of the room, leaving Sophie and Andrea on either side of Tom's bed. Sophie looked across at her friend and saw that Andrea was having as much of a struggle as she herself was to keep her emotions firmly under control.

CHAPTER SIX

'SO WHERE does this go?' Benedict held up a table lamp.

'Oh, sitting-room, please.' Sophie was sitting on the kitchen floor of her new apartment, surrounded by pots and pans and utensils. When she'd left her previous flat her possessions had been put into storage and now, on moving day, the men she'd hired had simply transported them to Clifton Court.

'Those curtains are a very good fit in the bedroom.' Andrea suddenly appeared, passing Benedict in the doorway. 'You'd think they'd been especially made.'

'I know. I've been lucky where curtains are concerned. The only new ones I'll have to buy are for the sitting-room—those windows are much larger than my last ones.' Sophie sat back on her heels and surveyed the boxes and packing cases around her. 'I can't believe I'm really here,' she said with a little sigh. 'It's all been so quick and it doesn't seem possible how smoothly it's all gone.'

'Ah, it makes all the difference if there's no chain when buying property,' said Benedict, appearing in the open doorway again, obviously having overheard what Sophie had just said. 'Also the fact that it's a brand-new property.'

'And not having to arrange a mortgage must help as well,' said Andrea. 'Honestly, Sophie, you don't know how lucky you are.'

'Oh, I do. I do,' replied Sophie with a laugh.

'I'm afraid I've got to go,' said Andrea. 'I'm on duty tonight. I'm doing an extra to boost my Christmas funds.'

Sophie scrambled to her feet. 'Thanks for helping, Andrea. I really appreciate it.'

'That's OK.' Andrea looked at Benedict and grinned. 'Isn't that what friends are for?'

'Absolutely.' He leaned against the doorframe and smiled. Dressed in a roll-necked grey sweater and black jeans, and with his dark hair even more tousled than usual, he, too, had worked tirelessly to help Sophie to get straight.

Sophie walked out into the corridor with Andrea. 'I'll see you on Monday,' she said.

'Yes, all right.' Andrea nodded as she headed for the lift, then she stopped and looked over her shoulder. 'When's Miles coming down?' she asked.

'Next weekend, he says.'

'Good. Does that mean a pre-Christmas flat-warming?'

'It might do,' Sophie replied, 'but even if there isn't time for that, he'll be here for the staff party.' As the lift doors closed on her friend she turned and made her way back into her flat. She found Benedict removing books from one of the packing cases. 'I think,' she said, 'that you've done quite enough for today.'

'Nonsense,' he replied briskly. 'Once it's done, it's done.'

'Yes, I know. But it's jolly tiring, this house-moving lark. How about I make us some more tea?'

'Now you're talking. Are these for the book-case in the sitting-room?'

She nodded, watching him as he carried her precious books off into the sitting-room, then with a little sigh she turned and filled the kettle.

Benedict and Andrea had both proved themselves to be really good friends, and Sophie
knew that Andrea was still hopeful that
Benedict might ask her out. Although there
was a part of Sophie that recoiled from that
situation, the sensible, common-sense side of
her told her it was probably the best thing that
could happen because she herself was still far
more aware of the new registrar than was good
for her. Maybe if his attentions were engaged
elsewhere, having him around would be easier.

And when all was said and done, she *would*
have to get used to him being around, not only
as a colleague but now also as a neighbour.
Since he'd come to work on the paediatric unit,
and because of the close nature of their work,
Sophie had come to know him pretty well, and
more and more she'd liked what she'd seen.
He obviously genuinely loved children—that
was apparent in his every word and gesture—
and she'd found a renewed rapport with him
with every child who came onto the ward.

At that moment the kettle began to boil and
Sophie brought her thoughts rapidly back to
the present as she brewed yet another pot of
tea. Carrying the teapot on a tray, together with

two mugs, a carton of milk and the remains of a packet of digestive biscuits into the sitting-room, she found Benedict studying the titles of her books before stacking them in her large pine bookcase.

'You seem to have everything here from *Swallows and Amazons* to *Madame Bovary*.' He looked up with a grin as she set the tray down on the top of an unopened tea chest.

'I suppose my tastes are pretty varied,' she replied with a laugh as she knelt on the carpet in front of the tea chest. 'And the other thing, of course, is that I can't bear to throw any books away. In this tea chest here...' she pointed to the one bearing the tea tray '...you'll find my *Bunty* annuals and my *Famous Five* books.'

'I'm hardly in a position to criticise that.' With a rueful grin Benedict lowered himself to the floor and sat with his hands loosely linked around his knees. 'At home in Norfolk I still have all the *Just William* books in the room that was my bedroom when I was a boy.'

'It looks like we shared a similar childhood,' said Sophie. 'I always had my nose in a book.

I read everything I could lay my hands on, from comics to the classics.'

'Me, too.' He watched her reflectively as she poured the tea.

Aware that his scrutiny was starting to make her nervous, she passed him his mug, which he set carefully down on the ornamental hearth, then offered him the packet of biscuits.

'Thanks.' He took one and bit into it, trying to catch the crumbs to prevent them from falling onto the carpet. 'Sorry,' he said, failing miserably.

'It's OK. I'll have to vacuum anyway when all this is packed away.' She waved a hand vaguely around the room then in an effort to prevent a silence, which she had the feeling might become uncomfortable, she said, 'Andrea was asking if I'd be having a flat-warming party before Christmas.'

'And will you?' He was about to take another mouthful but he paused, the biscuit poised halfway to his mouth, and looked at her, his eyebrows raised enquiringly.

'I don't know, I'll have to see,' she replied, without meeting his gaze. What she should have said was that it would depend on whether or not Miles was able to get down, but she didn't. Somehow Miles was the last person she wanted to talk about at that precise moment, just as she wouldn't have wanted to tell Benedict that the reason Andrea was so keen for her to have a flat-warming party was so that she, Andrea, could get to know the new registrar rather better.

Instead, they sat there together on the floor of her new flat, surrounded by her belongings, sipping tea and munching biscuits, satisfyingly at ease in each other's company.

The idyll was shattered some time later by the ringing of a phone.

Sophie looked up sharply and was about to scramble to her feet to look for her phone, which had somehow become submerged under packing paper, when with a grin Benedict pulled his mobile phone from his pocket.

'It's OK,' he said. 'It's mine. Hello? Oh, hello, Samir.' He pulled a face in Sophie's direction and she knew he feared he was about to be called in to work. Then his expression changed and grew serious. The hazel eyes darkened and the jaw tightened as he listened, and briefly the dark lashes swept his cheek and he inhaled deeply. 'Right,' he said at last. 'Thanks. Yes, yes, you're quite right, Samir. Thanks for letting me know.'

'Is everything all right?' Anxiously Sophie looked at him as he replaced the phone in his pocket.

He nodded. 'Samir thought I'd like to know—the police have just arrested a man in connection with the attacks on Tom Rowe and his family.'

Sophie's eyes widened and she grew very still. 'Who was it?' she asked quietly at last.

'The mother's boyfriend, apparently,' Benedict replied. 'It seems she'd finished her relationship with him a few days previously and had intended returning to her ex-husband.'

'That's what Tom's father said when he visited,' Sophie replied. 'There was skepticism at the time that it may have been a ploy on his part to deflect suspicion away from himself.' She paused, reflecting for a moment on the tall, rather studious-looking man who had been so devastated when he'd visited his son. 'I'm glad it wasn't him,' she said. 'Tom loves him so much.'

Benedict rose to his feet. 'What else would you like done?' he asked, looking around.

'I don't think there's a lot more that we can do today,' Sophie replied.

'What about those pictures?' He pointed to a stack of framed prints resting against the wall.

'I can't put those up yet. I don't have a drill, neither do I have any Rawlplugs. I thought that could be a job for my father when he has the time.'

'I've got a drill and Rawlplugs—I'll get them.'

'No, really, Benedict,' she protested. 'You've done quite enough today as it is.'

'It won't take long. I'll be back in a moment.' With that he was gone out of her flat and down the corridor to his own apartment.

Sophie carried the tray back to the kitchen and rinsed the mugs. She was about to go back to the sitting-room when she caught sight of the roller blind she'd used at her previous kitchen window poking out of the top of a large black plastic bag. Pulling it out completely, she held it up. Previously she'd thought it wouldn't fit but seeing it now, close to the window, she wondered if she might have been wrong.

Setting the blind down on the draining-board, she looked round and caught sight of her aluminium stepladder behind the kitchen door. Carefully she carried the ladder to the sink where she set it up. Then, picking up the blind, she ascended the ladder to the top step and, leaning across the sink and draining-board, held the blind against the window.

To her satisfaction, it fitted perfectly. With a little sigh of relief she began to descend the steps, and it was then that her foot slipped. Afterwards, she was to wonder exactly what had happened, whether her shoe had been loose, whether perhaps there had been some-thing slippery on that particular step of the lad-der or whether even, just briefly, she'd lost her balance, but at the time all she knew was a moment of panic as she teetered on the steps. And then, just as she might have fallen, strong arms went around her, restoring her balance.

'Steady on there,' a voice murmured against her ear. 'What do you think you're doing?'

'Oh!' She suddenly felt extremely foolish.
'I was only… I was just… The blind… I didn't
know whether it would fit…'

Benedict was still holding her when surely
he should have released her by now. Maybe
she should struggle, move smartly out of the
circle of his arms. Yes, that was definitely
what she should do.

So, if that was the case, why instead did she
do nothing of the sort? Why did she lean
against him, content to rest there awhile
against the firm contours of his body?

And then, as if that wasn't enough, why,
when he turned her gently to face him, did she
do nothing to stop him? And why, when he
finally released her, only for his hands to take
her face between them, did she still do nothing?

By the time his mouth had found hers, not
only was she not doing anything to stop him
but with parted lips and closed eyes, and with
her own arms creeping around his neck, she
was all but welcoming him. Because suddenly
it was as if this moment was what they'd both
been moving towards ever since they'd met,

ever since their eyes had met at that very first moment on the ward.

His lips were firm and cool, just as she'd known they would be, which, of course, meant that she *had* been waiting and anticipating this moment. Surely, for someone in her position, who was already committed in a relationship, wasn't that very wrong?

The last place she should be was in this man's arms, melting at his touch as he buried his fingers in her hair, when she knew that after he'd gone she would be waiting to hear from another as to when she would see him again.

She should pull away now, the voice of her conscience told her, end this madness before it went any further. But the temptation of the very thought of it going further was almost more than she could bear. The bedroom was very near—what if he guided her there? Would she resist then, tell him firmly he would have to go? Or would she wait until he'd undressed her? By then it would be too late because once she'd felt his skin against hers, his hands on her body, it would be way past the point of no return and all she would be capable of doing would be to abandon herself to his love-making...

'Sophie...? Cooee... Is there anyone there...? Oh, I say... Oh, I'm sorry...'

They sprang apart. Sophie spun round and to her dismay found her mother standing in the open doorway, a look of pure astonishment on her face. In her hands she carried what appeared to be a freshly baked pie.

'Oh!' Sophie gasped, red-faced with embarrassment and confusion. 'Oh, Mum, I wasn't expecting you.'

'Well, no, evidently.' Patricia Quentin recovered her composure quite rapidly. 'I thought you might be in need of some help.' Carefully she set the pie down on Sophie's coffee-table. 'But I can see you seem to have things pretty well under control.' Her gaze turned to Benedict, who was standing with one hand rubbing the back of his neck, the gesture somehow both boyish and embarrassed. 'So, aren't you going to introduce me?'

'Oh, yes,' said Sophie. 'Yes, of course. Mum, this is Benedict Lawrence. He's my... my neighbour.'

'Really?' There was open amusement now in her mother's eyes. 'I must say, you don't seem to have wasted any time in making the acquaintance of your neighbours.'

'Oh, he isn't *only* my neighbour—'

'Evidently.'

'No, Mum, you don't understand. Benedict is the registrar on Paediatrics. Benedict...' She turned, overcome with confusion and exasperation. 'This is my mother, Patricia Quentin.'

'How d'you do?' They shook hands and an embarrassed little silence followed. Then Benedict said, 'Well, if you don't mind, Sophie, I think I'd best be off.'

'Yes, of course. Thank you, Benedict, for all your help.' She began to follow him to the door.

'Don't mention it. I was glad I was able to help.' He paused and looked back at Sophie's mother. 'Nice to have met you, Mrs Quentin,' he said.

'And you, Mr Lawrence,' she replied drily.

At the outer door of the flat he turned and looked at Sophie. 'I'll see you later,' he said, his eyes once again full of amusement as they met hers.

'Yes, all right, Benedict,' she replied hastily.

It was only after she'd shut the door and had come back into the flat and caught sight of his drill and the packet of Rawlplugs that she remembered he'd been about to put up her pictures. She half turned to the door again with the idea of perhaps calling him back, then thought better of it and with a little sigh went back into the sitting-room to face her mother.

'Well, dear, I'm sorry if I interrupted something.' Patricia Quentin coolly raised her eyebrows.

'No, Mum, you didn't interrupt anything,' said Sophie with a sigh.

Suddenly she felt unbearably weary, as if the events of the day—the house move and all that had entailed, and the tension and excitement of the last half-hour—had suddenly caught up with her and overwhelmed her in a great wave of tiredness.

'Well, it certainly didn't look that way when I came in...'

'Mum, believe me, it was nothing.'

'It didn't look like nothing from where I was standing.'

'Well, I can assure you it was. It was just one of those things that happened. It wasn't planned—it was completely spontaneous.'

'He seems very nice.'

'Yes, he is very nice,' Sophie agreed.

'Is he single?'

'Yes, as far as I know.'

'And was it him who told you about this place? You did say he's a neighbour?'

'Yes, he lives down the corridor and, yes, it was him who told me this place was back on the market. I would probably never have known about it otherwise.'

'So he's been helping you today?' Her mother looked round the room.

Sophie nodded. 'Yes, he has, and Andrea was here as well. They've both worked very hard. I'm very grateful to them.'

'Yes, I'm sure,' murmured her mother.

An awkward silence fell between them, then Patricia Quentin said, 'Tell me, dear, does your new friend Benedict know about Miles?'

'No, Mum, he doesn't,' Sophie replied patiently, but she found herself biting her lip.

'Do you have any plans to tell him?'

'Why?' she demanded. 'Why should I?'

'Well, from where I was standing, and from what I saw when I came in, I would say I rather think you should.'

Sophie drew in her breath. 'There's nothing going on, Mum,' she said sharply.

'Darling, I wasn't for one moment suggesting there was.' Patricia looked shocked and just for the moment Sophie couldn't decide whether it was feigned or not.

'No, well…' she said defensively.

'On the other hand,' her mother began, then hesitated. 'Maybe if you're thinking there's no reason to tell Mr Lawrence about Miles,' she went on after a moment, 'then maybe you should be considering the alternative.'

'Whatever do you mean?' Sophie's eyes narrowed as she stared at her mother.

'Well, maybe you should be telling Miles about Mr Lawrence,' Patricia replied coolly. 'Now, tell me, dear, shall I put this apple pie in your fridge or shall we have a slice now? I don't have any cream, I'm afraid…'

'You never have liked Miles.' There was a flat, accusing note in Sophie's voice now as she faced her mother across the coffee-table.

'Darling,' her mother protested, 'whatever do you mean? We did our utmost, your father and I, to make Miles welcome when he came down to see you.'

'I know you did and that may well be the case,' Sophie replied, 'but it doesn't alter the fact that you don't particularly like him. Come on, Mum, you can't fool me. I know you too well. I know your every expression and I know when you're pretending.'

When her mother remained silent Sophie went right on. 'So come on, tell me,' she demanded, 'what is it about Miles that you don't like? Is it simply that he isn't a doctor, and you had your heart set on a doctor for me?'

'Of course not!' Her mother sounded genuinely shocked now. 'That makes me sound a dreadful snob!'

'Sorry.' Sophie had the grace to look a little shame-faced. 'I didn't mean it to sound quite like that. But if it isn't that, what is it? Come on, tell me.'

'I'm not sure I'd go so far as to say I don't actually like him,' said her mother slowly. 'But you know how I always seem to have this sixth sense about people...?'

'Yes, we know...' Sophie gave a short laugh. Her mother's sixth sense and intuitive powers were well known in the Quentin household.

'You have to admit, in the past I've often been right,' her mother protested.

'Yes, all right,' Sophie grudgingly agreed. 'So go on, then, tell me—what has your intuition told you about Miles?'

'Nothing specific...' Her mother began to look uncomfortable, as if she regretted even starting this particular conversation. 'Just a feeling really. There's something about him I can't quite fathom, that's all.'

'And what did your "first impression" intuition tell you about Benedict Lawrence?' asked Sophie with a trace of sarcasm.

'That he's straight, honest and utterly uncomplicated,' Patricia replied unhesitatingly.

'Now, how did I know that was what you were going to say?' Sophie laughed. 'Maybe it was because I know that you're fully aware that a paediatric registrar eventually becomes a paediatric consultant.'

'Sophie, please!'

'Or, on the other hand, are you merely implying that Miles is none of those things?'

'Oh, I don't know, darling, really I don't,' her mother protested. 'Like I said, it was just a feeling that there was something about him he was holding back, something he didn't want us to know.' She paused. 'When's he coming down again?' she said at last.

'At the weekend, I hope,' Sophie replied casually.

'So not actually at Christmas?'

Sophie shook her head. 'There's no point really. I shall be working and, besides, there's his father to think about. He can't just leave him—especially at Christmas. And let's face it, Mum, if he did, you really would have something to say about him, wouldn't you?'

'Oh, dear, I wish now I hadn't said anything at all,' said Patricia ruefully.

They dropped the subject of Miles Fraser, and of Benedict Lawrence, after that, instead enjoying a slice of the mouth-watering apple pie and a glass of white wine. But after her mother had completed a tour of the flat and had gone, and as Sophie wandered around her new home, setting things straight and revelling in the fact that it was all hers and that she was independent once more, her thoughts turned again to the conversation they'd had.

She'd long suspected that her mother wasn't too enthralled with Miles, so that particular aspect of things hadn't come as too much of a surprise. What had bothered her more was the fact that her mother should have deemed it necessary for her to tell Benedict about her relationship with Miles. In her heart Sophie had already suspected that the moment would come when she would have to do so, but for her mother to have considered it a necessity made her think about the conclusions she must have reached in that moment she'd seen Benedict and herself together.

But it had only been a kiss, for heaven's sake. What was a kiss? Nothing. A simple, spontaneous gesture of affection between two friends, that's all.

So, if that's all it was, why did she feel faint every time she thought about it? Why had she been so exasperated when her mother had arrived at the precise moment she had? And why now, several hours after the event, was she having to fight the almost uncontrollable urge to dash down the corridor to Benedict's flat, to hurl herself into his arms and to beg him to finish what he'd started?

CHAPTER SEVEN

'TOM'S much better, isn't he, Nurse Sophie?'

'Yes, Antonia, he is. Much better,' Sophie replied.

'Does that mean he'll be going home soon?' She detected a slight note of anxiety in the child's voice.

'No, not for some time yet.' She stopped beside Antonia's bed. 'What's that you're doing?' she asked, leaning across the table that spanned the bed.

'I'm making Christmas cards,' said Antonia. 'Look.'

'They're very nice,' said Sophie admiringly. 'I like that one there, with the angel talking to the shepherds.'

'That's for Fleur.' Antonia sounded pleased. 'Will you post them for me when I've finished?'

'Of course I will.'

'I could give them to Mummy but I don't want any of them to know. They won't be expecting to get cards from me this year,' said Antonia with a little giggle. 'They'll be really surprised.' She looked up suddenly, her coloured pencil poised in the air. 'Who's the new boy?' she asked, glancing down the ward to where curtains were drawn around a cubicle.

'That's Nathan,' Sophie replied. 'He's come to stay with us for a while for what we call a respite stay—to give his parents a break.'

'He's got cerebral palsy, hasn't he?' said Antonia, returning to her colouring.

'How did you know that?' Sophie looked at her in amazement.

'I just guessed,' Antonia replied with a shrug. 'He looks the same as another boy who was in here once before with me.'

As Sophie moved on down the ward, not for the first time she found herself marvelling at how much children picked up on a ward just from day-to-day routine. And it seemed Antonia had picked up more than most after her many prolonged visits.

A couple of days previously Tom Rowe had been moved from the side ward into the main ward and that morning he was seated in a large chair beside his bed, propped up by pillows as he watched a favourite video. It was true, what Antonia had just said—he was looking better in spite of still not having spoken a word. His injuries were healing and his bruises fading from purple to yellow smudges. He was so engrossed in the antics of the characters from *The Jungle Book* on the screen that he hardly seemed aware of Sophie's presence so, after checking his observation chart, she carried on to the nurses' station.

Sister Bailey looked out of her office as Sophie approached and beckoned her inside. 'I just wanted to give you a briefing on Nathan,' she said. 'He's been having epileptic fits, that's what prompted his admission to the ward. His parents are understandably exhausted. He had the last fit as he was being admitted. He's sleeping now. As you know from his last admission, he's quite incapable of doing anything for himself and that includes feeding, washing and dressing.

'He's also unable to play alone. I've drawn up a care plan for him but I still need to contact the physiotherapist and the speech therapist, who will need to see him on a regular basis. I think I'll also have a word with the occupational therapist to see if she can devise some sort of play that might hold his attention.'

'Is it going to be possible to keep him on the main ward?' asked Sophie.

'I doubt it, at least not at night-time. He'll probably prove too disruptive for the other children, but the side wards weren't free when he came in last night. However, young Michelle will be going home today so we'll be able to move him in there tonight. We must make sure, though, that he's brought into the main ward during the day. It's essential that there's communication and that he can feel part of all that's going on.' Sister paused and consulted a list on her desk. 'Now, I think that's all for the moment,' she said. 'Oh, no, wait a moment. Baby Reynolds—is she ready for her operation?'

'Yes.' Sophie nodded. 'Andrea is with her—' She broke off as Sister Bailey suddenly looked out onto the ward.

'Oh, there's Dr Lawrence,' she said, a note of relief in her voice. 'That's good. I need him to adjust Nathan's medication.'

At the sudden mention of his name Sophie felt her heart leap painfully against her ribs.

She hadn't seen him yet that morning and he hadn't returned to her flat the previous day after her mother had gone. Somehow she'd restrained herself from going to see him but she'd spent a near sleepless night of turmoil. She now found herself wondering quite how he would react after the embarrassing incident of the day before.

She didn't have to wonder for long because, catching Sister Bailey's eye, he came straight into the office. At that moment, however, the phone rang, and as Sister answered it she turned away to take some notes, leaving Sophie to face the registrar.

'Hi,' he said softly, his gaze meeting and holding hers.

'Hello.' She nodded.

'Do I need to apologise?' He spoke in the same soft tone, not that there was any need to worry about Sister overhearing for she was deep in conversation with whoever was on the phone.

'Apologise?' asked Sophie faintly.

'Yes, for putting you in a compromising situation in front of your mother.'

'Er, no.' She felt the colour flood her face and uncomfortably knew that he saw it. 'That won't be necessary.'

'In that case, the least I can do is to come back and finish what I was doing.'

She stared at him in astonishment.

'Your pictures...?' he said.

'Oh, the pictures. Oh, yes, of course.'

'What did you think I meant?' His eyes were full of amusement now and she was forced to look away.

'Nothing,' she muttered.

'So would this evening be all right?'

'Er, yes. That will be fine...thank you,' she heard herself say.

'I didn't quite dare come back last evening,' he said with a grin. 'I thought your mum might still be there and I didn't quite know what she'd make of it if I turned up again.'

Much to Sophie's relief, Sister Bailey put the phone down at that moment and turned to them. 'Sheer incompetence, that's what it is,' she snapped, obviously referring to whomever she had been talking to. 'Now, where was I?'

'Nathan's medication?' said Sophie.

'Oh, yes, that's right. Nathan Briggs, the cerebral palsy patient. Could you look at his medication, please, Dr Lawrence? He's currently on phenytoin sodium in suspension form, but I gather Mr Crowley-Smith wants the dose increased in view of Nathan's recent epileptic fits.'

'Of course.' Benedict moved across to Sister's desk where he authorised the boy's medication sheet. When he'd finished he straightened up. 'I think I'd like to take a look at him,' he said.

'Nurse Quentin will take you down there,' replied Sister Bailey.

'Thanks.' Benedict nodded. 'Oh, how is Antonia this morning?' he added.

'She's busy making her Christmas cards at the moment,' replied Sophie.

'She gets exhausted very quickly,' Sister added.

'Any pain?'

'Not really.' Sister shook her head. 'Some discomfort from time to time but we keep that under control.'

'I'll take a look at her as well.' Benedict replied. 'Then I have to get down to Theatre.

I understand you have a baby for us this morning with pyloric stenosis.'

'Yes, a little girl—Tamara Reynolds. She's
all ready for Theatre.'

'Right, let's go. Thank you, Sister.' He nodded at Sister Bailey then followed Sophie onto
the ward.

She was more aware of him than ever now,
and as they walked side by side down the ward
to Nathan's bed Sophie resolved there and then
that when he came that evening she would
have to tell him that she was already in a relationship. She couldn't have him thinking,
even for one moment, that they could carry on
where they'd left off the previous day. She
would have to make him understand that what
had happened had been a moment of madness,
an unguarded moment, and quite definitely not
one to be repeated.

They found Nathan had woken up when
they stopped at the foot of his bed. Mollie was
with him and he was protesting loudly at finding himself in unfamiliar surroundings.

'I can't get his attention,' said Mollie as the
boy continued to thrash around in the bed.

Benedict looked round the ward until in the play area his gaze fell on a brightly coloured mobile of different kinds of fish. Walking across to it, he lifted it from its hook and returned to Nathan.

'Let me try,' he said. Positioning himself directly in front of the boy, he endeavoured to establish eye contact with him. This proved difficult as Nathan was tossing his head from side to side. At last, however, Benedict succeeded in gaining the child's attention and immediately lifted the mobile in front of his eyes. This seemed to mesmerise him and he grew quieter with only the occasional spasm that shook his body.

'Well done, Dr Lawrence,' said Mollie. 'You must have a magic touch. You wouldn't like to stay up here, by any chance, would you? I've a feeling we're going to have our work cut out.'

'I'll give you a hand in a moment, Mollie,' said Sophie as Benedict secured the mobile above Nathan's bed. 'I think it's going to take two of us to feed him and to wash him.'

'Oh, at least,' Mollie replied.

'Do you have a personal stereo in here?' asked Benedict suddenly.

'No, I don't think we have.' Sophie looked at Mollie who shook her head.

'He might like that,' said Benedict thoughtfully. 'I'll look out for one.'

They left Nathan, still watching the mobile, and moved on down the ward to Antonia. The little girl was asleep, however, her Christmas cards and coloured pencils strewn around her.

'Don't disturb her,' said Benedict softly. 'She needs her rest.'

They watched the sleeping child for a moment and Sophie felt a tug at her heartstrings as she noted Antonia's increased pallor that morning. It hadn't been so noticeable when Sophie had been talking to her earlier but now, as she slept, her fair skin looked almost transparent, the blue veins clearly visible.

After a moment or two they moved on, and as they came to Tom's bed Sophie saw that his video had finished. Benedict crouched down in front of the boy's chair. 'Hello, there, young man. How are you this morning?'

Tom nodded, and to Sophie's satisfaction she noticed that he didn't flinch away from

Benedict, as he had been doing up until then if anyone approached him, especially a male. But he still hadn't uttered a word since being admitted.

Benedict picked up the empty video case and looked at it. 'Oh, brilliant,' he said. 'My favourite. Who do you like best?'

Tom continued to stare at him in silence.

'My favourite is Baloo,' Benedict went on. 'I think he's really cool. I love that bit where he's floating down the river with Mowgli riding on his tummy, then those pesky monkeys whisk Mowgli away.'

Sophie was watching Tom carefully and she saw the expression in his eyes change and become more interested.

'Do you think,' Benedict said solemnly, 'that if I was to come back later I could watch a bit of this with you?' He glanced down at the video cover as he spoke.

Tom nodded eagerly and Benedict straightened up, ruffled the boy's hair and together with Sophie started to move away.

They'd only gone a few steps when Tom suddenly made a noise in his throat.

They both stopped and turned.

'King Louis,' he said, his voice hoarse and a little gruff. 'He's my favourite.'

Benedict and Sophie looked at each other in silent triumph. 'Good on you,' said Benedict with a chuckle. 'The King of the Swingers!'

'And who, may I ask, is King Louis?' asked Sophie, with a sideways glance at Benedict as they continued their way down the ward to the babies' section.

'You mean, you don't know?' Benedict stared at her in mock horror. 'I thought every-one knew who King Louis was.'

'Well, I'm afraid you've found one who doesn't.'

'I can see I shall have to do something about that. I suggest you come with me when I watch Tom's video with him.'

'So how come you're so up on children's videos?' asked Sophie with a laugh.

'They aren't only for children,' he protested solemnly, then, when he caught sight of her expression, he laughed. 'I have nephews and nieces in Norfolk. They keep me fully edu-cated in these matters.'

This was another facet to his life and sud-denly Sophie wanted to pursue it, wanted to know more about these unknown nephews and nieces with whom Benedict seemed to share a close relationship. And presumably, if there were children there had to be parents, parents who would be Benedict's siblings, and she wanted to know about those as well. She wanted to know everything about him, everything about the life he'd led before coming to St Winifred's. But she had no right even to ask, she knew that.

They stopped in front of Tamara Reynolds's cot where Cheryl, a care assistant, was caring for the baby before she was taken down to Theatre.

'What's her history?' asked Benedict as he picked up Tamara's observation chart.

'Problems with feeding almost since birth,' Sophie replied, 'then, more recently, projectile vomiting after two out of three feeds. She was dehydrated when she was first admitted. This has now been corrected and she's been prepared for this morning's theatre list.' As she finished speaking she watched as Benedict replaced the observation chart and leaned over the side of the cot, stretching out his hand towards the baby. Almost immediately the infant's tiny hand curled around Benedict's index finger.

He remained there for a few moments, before gently extricating himself from the baby's grip and returning with Sophie to the nurses' station.

'I need to get down and scrubbed up now,' he said, glancing at the clock above the main desk. He paused and looked at Sophie. 'What time this evening?' he asked.

'Come early,' she heard herself say. 'About six thirty. Then, after you've done the pictures, maybe you'd like a bite of supper.'

'That would be lovely.' His gaze met hers. 'I'll see you later, then.'

She didn't really know why she'd issued the supper invitation. Somehow the words had just seemed to have come out of her mouth. Probably it had been a very foolish thing to do in view of what had happened the previous evening. She should be discouraging—not encouraging—him.

On the other hand, surely there was nothing to say she couldn't invite a friend for supper, and there was no earthly reason why she and

Benedict shouldn't remain friends—even after she'd told him about Miles.

Sophie had little more time during her shift to think of relationships, friendships, Miles, or even Benedict himself, come to that, as the demands of the ward took over.

There was much to be done for Nathan, and once he'd been bathed and fed the physiotherapist arrived and the boy's poor, twisted little limbs were put through a full range of movements to help to keep them supple. Luckily, Nathan himself didn't seem to object to this, even apparently enjoying it in his own limited way. While the physiotherapist was still with him Tamara Reynolds came back from Theatre and her post-operative care plan was put into operation.

Since Tom Rowe had uttered those first few words to Benedict it seemed the floodgates had opened and he'd been unable to stop. He'd asked for his chair to be moved nearer to Antonia's bed and the two of them had chattered non-stop while Antonia finished her Christmas cards. And after lunch, when Benedict came back onto the ward to watch part of *The Jungle Book* with Tom, it wasn't only Sophie who joined them but Antonia as well.

'Well, I think that was brilliant,' said Benedict afterwards. 'Old Baloo the bear was every bit as good as I remember him.'

Antonia looked at Tom. 'Have you seen *One Hundred and One Dalmatians*?' she demanded.

'No, I don't think so...' he replied.

'We've got it at home. I'll ask Fleur to bring it in then we can all watch it. Oh, Sophie.' She looked up. 'I've finished my Christmas cards. You will post them for me, won't you?'

Sophie nodded. 'Yes, of course I will. I wish I'd written all my cards. I'm all behind this year.'

'It isn't long till Christmas, is it?' said Tom.

Sophie noticed the anxiety in the boy's voice. 'No,' she replied. 'Not long now.'

'What do you want for Christmas, Tom?' asked Benedict.

'A Star Wars game,' said Tom unhesitatingly.

'And what about you, Antonia?' Sophie turned to the girl in the bed. 'What do you want?'

'Well...' Antonia considered. 'I'd like some new ballet shoes really.' She shrugged as if that idea was really rather pointless, then more brightly she added, 'But what I'd really like, more than anything else, is to go home.'

Sophie swallowed and glanced at Benedict, but they were saved from answering by Tom who said, 'I'd like to go home, too, but I don't think I'll be able to. I don't think my mum will be well by then, or my sister... But I might go with my dad...' He cheered up considerably at the thought.

'What about you, Sophie?' asked Antonia. 'What would you like for Christmas?'

'I guess you could say I've already had my Christmas present,' Sophie replied.

'Oh, what was it? Tell me, please,' Antonia begged.

'Well, my grandmother died recently,' said Sophie. 'She left me some money and I've just bought myself a flat, so you could say I've been very lucky indeed this Christmas.' As she spoke her gaze met Benedict's, and she found herself looking quickly away as she wondered what he was thinking and, indeed, what his answer would be should Antonia ask him the same question.

Not allowing a chance to find out, she hastily changed the subject. 'Would you go and see baby Tamara now, please, Dr Lawrence?' she said.

While Benedict moved away down the ward to talk to the baby's parents, Sophie made her way to Nathan's cubicle, where he was engaged in some activity with the play therapist which involved fitting large, brightly-coloured shapes into corresponding holes in a plastic frame.

'How's he doing—?' Sophie began, then broke off abruptly as Nathan aimlessly threw one of the shapes, narrowly missing her head.

'He gets bored very quickly,' replied Julie, the therapist. 'It takes a long time to gain his attention and then when you have it he's ready to move on to the next thing.'

'Dr Lawrence seemed to hold his attention for a while with that mobile.' Sophie pointed to the brightly coloured fish.

'I may just try that again,' Julie replied. 'If it doesn't work, ask Dr Lawrence to come back, will you? He may have a few more good ideas.'

With a chuckle Sophie made her way back to the nurses' station, where she found Sister Bailey discussing the latest developments in the Rowe affair with Rosemary Lennard.

'So, let me get this straight,' Rosemary was saying. 'You're telling me that the police have actually charged this guy with the attack?'

'Apparently so.' Sister Bailey nodded.

'And he was the mother's boyfriend? So had he actually been living with the family?'

'We believe so. It seems he moved in shortly after Tom's father left which was about six months ago. My guess is that Tina Rowe, Tom's mother, soon discovered that he was a bit handy with his fists. She asked him to leave which, I gather, he did. Unfortunately he came back…and we know the rest,' she added grimly.

'How is Tina?' asked Sophie.

'She's coming along slowly,' Rosemary replied, 'but her injuries were pretty extensive.'

'And the little girl—Sara?'

'Yes, she's recovered very well. Social Services are talking about placing her in foster-care for a while.' She paused. 'Sister has just been telling me that Tom has spoken at last.'

Sophie nodded. 'Yes, we have Dr Lawrence to thank for that,' she replied. 'He took an interest in something that Tom was intensely interested in himself.'

'Good.' Rosemary nodded. 'Best thing that could have happened.'

'Tom was talking just now about spending Christmas with his father—do you think that will be possible?'

'It may be. Tom seems very fond of his father and there's no denying Peter Rowe's feelings for his children.'

'Were Tina and Peter really thinking of getting back together again?' Sophie looked from Rosemary to Hazel Bailey.

'Well, that's certainly what Peter told me when he visited Tom yesterday after the police had made their arrest.' Sister Bailey picked up a large pile of folders and turned as if to go back into her office, then suddenly she stopped and looked at Sophie. 'Talking of yesterday,' she said, 'wasn't it yesterday that you moved into your new apartment?'

Sophie smiled. 'Yes,' she replied, 'it was.'

'Sorry,' said Sister Bailey. 'I quite forgot. How did it go?'

'Pretty well as moves go.' Sophie nodded. 'I suppose it helped, having my furniture and belongings in store…and I did have plenty of assistance. Andrea came over, and so did Benedict. Oh, and my mother arrived, although I'm not sure that wasn't more of a hindrance than a help.'

Rosemary laughed, and as Sister Bailey disappeared into her office she said curiously, 'When you say that Benedict helped you, do you mean Dr Lawrence?'

Sophie nodded. 'Yes,' she said, 'he has an apartment in the same complex.'

'Ah,' said Rosemary. 'I thought you must have meant him. There can't be too many Benedicts around.' She paused. 'He's nice, isn't he?'

'Yes,' Sophie agreed, 'he is. Very nice. And the children adore him.'

'And he's so good with them. Should have a family of his own, a man like that. I must say there's been a bit of speculation about him up in our staffroom.'

'Oh, really?' asked Sophie. 'In what way?'

'Well, whether or not he has a woman tucked away up there in Suffolk or wherever it is he hails from.'

'Norfolk, actually,' Sophie replied.

'Yes, well, whatever.' Rosemary shrugged then, leaning forward a little, peered at Sophie. 'You seem to know quite a bit about him,' she said.

'Not really.' It was Sophie's turn to shrug, trying to appear casual. 'No more than anyone else.'

To her relief Rosemary seemed to accept that. It really wouldn't do for her to know that Benedict was in actual fact going to have supper with her that night in her new apartment. That really would have given them something to speculate about upstairs in the consultants' staffroom, and Sophie wasn't at all sure she either wanted, or even should be, the cause of any such speculation.

CHAPTER EIGHT

IT HAD to be something fairly simple for supper because Sophie wasn't too organised yet, having only just moved into her apartment. On the way home from work she bought a couple of tuna steaks, enough ingredients to make a yoghurt and cucumber sauce and a salad, a French loaf and a bottle of Chardonnay.

It was pure delight to go home to the apartment, kick off her shoes, take a shower, unwind and wander through the rooms, knowing it was all hers. Sophie loved her independence. Grateful though she'd been to her parents for allowing her to return to her old home for a while, there had been times when she'd longed for her own place again.

After she'd showered and changed into a sweater and trousers, she set about preparing supper. While she was washing the salad the doorbell rang, and she felt a stab of something she could only really describe as excitement, which was ridiculous really, she told herself firmly as she hurried to answer the door. After all, this was simply a neighbour doing a kindness and being repaid for his trouble by yet another kindness.

Benedict was leaning against the doorframe when she opened the door, and as his gaze met hers she felt her heart give that now all too familiar little lurch. He was wearing a dark green cord shirt which seemed to accentuate the flecks in his eyes, making them appear more green than hazel.

'Hi,' he said. 'Did I by any chance happen to leave my drill here last night?'

She laughed. 'Well, I've heard some chat-up lines in my life…but, yes, you did leave your drill here.' Standing aside, she allowed him to enter the hallway. Closing the door, she eased past him, only too conscious of the merriment in his eyes, and led the way into her sitting-room.

He stood for a moment, arms akimbo, looking round at the bare walls. 'Have you had time to decide where you want these pictures?' he asked.

'Yes,' she replied. 'As you'll see, I've placed each picture against the wall it's intended for.'

'Right.' He nodded. 'If we can just make a pencil mark for height and position, I can get on.'

Fifteen minutes later Sophie was back in the kitchen, and to the accompaniment of the harsh, but at the same time oddly comforting sound of drilling she completed her preparation of supper.

At last Benedict appeared in the kitchen doorway. 'All done,' he said. 'Come and look.'

She followed him—first into the sitting-room, then to the hall, followed by the bathroom and finally into her bedroom, where her print of lavender fields in the Dordogne hung above her bed.

'They look lovely,' she exclaimed happily. 'Thank you so much, Benedict. It really feels like home now.'

'Happy to oblige, ma'am.' Playfully he tugged at his forelock.

'I'm sure if you go to the kitchens, Cook will find you a crust,' said Sophie, impulsively playing the same game as him. As they reached the kitchen, she turned and said, 'Would you like a glass of wine?'

'Love one. Thanks.'

As she poured the wine she was only too aware of his eyes on her, and suddenly she found herself wishing that things were different, that this was simply the start of a friendship that could develop naturally, instead of her having to tell him that this was as far as it could go. Then she pulled herself up sharply. What in the world was she thinking of? She had Miles, for heaven's sake, and he didn't deserve this.

Turning, she handed Benedict his glass then picked up her own.

Not giving her the chance to say anything, he raised his own glass. 'Cheers,' he said. 'To you and your new home.'

They both took a sip of their wine then, as Sophie put her glass down on the worktop and turned back to the stove where the steaks were slowly grilling, Benedict leaned against the draining-board, his long legs thrust out before him. 'Did you see the list for the Christmas activities today?' he asked suddenly. 'Or had you gone by then?'

'No, I didn't see it.' Sophie shook her head. 'Who put it up?'

'Sister Bailey, as far as I know. I only happened to see it when I nipped back to the ward with a Walkman for Nathan.'

'You found a Walkman?' She looked up quickly. 'That's marvellous! What did Nathan make of it?'

'Well, it was strange really,' Benedict mused. 'We tried some children's tapes—you know, nursery rhymes that sort of thing—and he didn't seem bothered. Not so much as a flicker of interest. Then we tried pop music, with much the same result. It wasn't until we tried some of Sister Bailey's classical tapes that we got his attention. He loved the *1812 Overture* and when I left he was listening quite happily to a tape of operatic arias.'

'Amazing,' said Sophie. 'On the other hand, maybe that's what he hears at home and it was simply familiar to him.'

'Who knows?' Benedict shrugged.

'Still, it was good of you to take the trouble.'

'Least I could do, really. Poor little chap—he can't have much pleasure.'

'It was still good of you,' Sophie insisted. 'I don't know many registrars who would go to that trouble. In fact, now that I think of it, I couldn't name one other…' She threw him a glance and saw that he looked rather embarrassed. 'So, what about this Christmas list?' she asked, changing the subject.

'Oh, yes.' He nodded. 'Well, the staff party is this weekend in the social club—but you probably knew that anyway.' When Sophie nodded he carried on. 'The children's party with Father Christmas is on the ward on the 23rd of December, then on Christmas Eve we're to have carols around the tree. On Christmas morning there'll be another visit from Father Christmas—alias Franklin Crowley-Smith—then as many staff as possible will join the children for Christmas lunch.'

'All fairly predictable,' said Sophie, as she tossed the salad then carried the bowl together with the cucumber sauce to the table in the dining alcove.

'Does Franklin dress up every year?'

She nodded. 'Yes, for as long as he's been at St Winifred's. Before that it was the previous consultant. I guess it's a sort of tradition.' She paused. 'If you're ready, we can eat.'

'Wonderful. I'm starving—but, then, that's nothing new because I usually am.' Pushing himself away from the draining-board, Benedict strolled into the alcove where Sophie had placed a bowl of floating candles on the table.

When he was seated she carried the plates with the tuna steaks from the kitchen, setting one before him and the other in her own place.

'Help yourself to bread and salad.' Leaning across the table, she poured the Chardonnay.

'This looks excellent,' he said, eyeing the food. 'You obviously enjoy cooking.'

'Yes, I suppose I do.' Sophie nodded. 'But this is pretty basic stuff tonight, I'm afraid. I haven't really got my act together yet.'

'It doesn't look basic to me.' He took his first mouthful. 'I'm impressed and this sauce is delicious—you'll have to let me in on the secret.'

Sophie felt her cheeks growing warm at all this praise and decided to change the subject.

'Tell me,' she said between mouthfuls, 'these nephews and nieces of yours—how many are there, and do you have brothers or sisters?'

He laughed. 'Both. I have two sisters and one brother.'

'Really?' She was surprised. She hadn't imagined him coming from a large family. 'Are they older or younger than you?'

'One sister, Catherine, and my brother Joe are older, my other sister, Theresa, is two years younger than me. They're all married. Catherine has two sons, Joe has three daughters and Theresa has twin daughters and she's just had a little boy whom she's named Benedict—after me, she says, because she's beginning to despair that I'll ever get married.' He laughed. 'I told her I'll get married when I'm good and ready and when I meet the woman I want to spend the rest of my life with.'

His eyes met Sophie's as he finished talking and at the expression she saw there she felt a little thrill flutter the length of her spine. This was dangerous talk, even more disconcerting than praising her cooking, and once again she found herself searching for an alternative subject, but even as she floundered he spoke again, giving her no chance.

'I thought I'd found that woman once,' he said quietly.

'Really?' Sophie's voice came out husky and she coughed, clearing her throat, 'Really?' she said again.

'Yes.' He nodded. 'She was a nurse. We worked together for a time. She took me home to meet her parents, I took her home to meet mine. Everything seemed fine, everyone liked each other...'

'But?'

'I guess there just wasn't enough magic there in the end. We wanted different things from life. I wanted a family, she didn't. I wanted to stay in this country, she wanted to work abroad. If the magic had been right those things could have been overcome. As it was...'

He shrugged and trailed off, leaving the sentence unfinished, but Sophie found herself wanting to know more about this unknown woman with whom at one time Benedict had thought he'd wanted to spend the rest of his life. Which was ridiculous really because, after all, what could it possibly have to do with her?

And then, to her horror, she heard herself say, 'What was her name?' She didn't know why she said it, because it was the last thing she wanted to know.

'Danielle,' he replied. 'She was half-French,' he added, and for Sophie the far-away look in his eyes conjured up an image of a sultry, sun-kissed blonde to whom already, without having met her, she'd unreasonably taken an immediate aversion.

It was his turn then to change the subject. 'But that's enough about me.' He leaned forward slightly across the table and the light from the candles lit his features, giving them a slightly surreal appearance. 'What about you?'

'Me?' replied Sophie in alarm. Whatever did he want to know about her?

'Yes.' Calmly, totally unaware of the sudden thumping of her heart, he added, 'I know hardly anything about you.'

She swallowed. 'What do you want to know?'

'Well, for a start, do you have brothers and sisters?'

'I have one brother,' she replied. 'His name is Ashley—he's a radiologist and he's nearly four years older than me.'

'And is he married?'

She nodded. 'Yes, he and his wife Jennifer live in Scotland. They have one little girl, Daisy, and Jennifer is expecting another baby in the spring.'

'And what about you?' His voice softened suddenly.

'Me?' His gaze had sought hers and held it almost against her will as she found it utterly impossible to look away.

'Yes, do your plans for the future include marriage and children?'

'Oh, yes. Yes, of course…eventually.'

'Presumably, when you, too, meet the right person.' He paused. In the silence Sophie was convinced he must now hear the hammering of her heart. 'Unless, of course,' he went on, 'you've already done so…?'

Suddenly she could bear the secrecy no longer. She knew that now was the moment she ought to tell him about Miles. But still she found it impossible to do so. If she did, the magic of the evening would be over, the spell would be broken, and she didn't want that to happen—not yet. Maybe it was wrong, but reality would come soon enough and she wanted this moment to last. She wanted to savour it, to go on enjoying his company.

So, instead of answering his question, she merely evaded it. Instead, she simply smiled in enigmatic fashion, refilling first his glass and then her own and saying, 'In case you're wondering, my brother didn't miss out over our grandmother's legacy. We each received a half-share and our father inherited her house.'

'I hadn't wondered.' He looked surprised at her sudden change of tack. 'But now you come to mention it, I dare say I might have wondered as I got to know you better. But maybe I would have simply reached the conclusion that you were your grandmother's favourite…and that wouldn't be too difficult to imagine.' He laughed and Sophie flushed.

'No,' she said hastily, 'nothing like that at all. My grandmother was a wealthy woman. Her husband, my late grandfather, made a lot of money from stocks and shares.'

'And their foresight has now enabled you to buy this.' He glanced around as he spoke.

'Yes, and I'm more than grateful. Believe me. In the normal course of events I could never have afforded anything like this. My last flat was rented, and on a bad month I was sometimes hard pushed just to make ends meet. This is like a dream come true.'

They sat on, talking, as the floating candles burnt down, spluttered, then one by one began to go out. They talked of everything, from their work to their childhoods—his in Norfolk in the rambling old farmhouse that was still the family home, and hers in Hampshire.

'My father's family were in farming,' he said in answer to one of her questions. 'He's retired now, but my brother still farms and my elder sister is married to a farmer.'

'What about holidays? Did you go away as children?'

'We always went to my mother's family in Ireland. She comes from County Kerry.'

'I hadn't realised you were half-Irish.' Sophie sat back in her chair and surveyed him with renewed interest.

'Oh, yes,' he answered, slipping into a strong Irish accent. 'Had you not recognised our saintly names? Only a saint's name would be good enough for any child of my mother.'

'Now that you mention it...' Sophie joined in his laughter.

'What about you?' he asked. 'Did you go on family holidays?'

'We had a cottage on the west coast of Scotland, which belonged to my grandparents. We always went there. It was where my brother Ashley met his wife.'

'And what about you?'

'Me?' She looked up, wondering what he meant.

'Yes, was there no handsome Scotsman for you?' As he spoke the last candle spluttered and went out. Sophie rose quickly to her feet as they were left in semi-darkness, with only the light from the kitchen shining into the dining alcove. 'Oh,' she said. 'Oh, no, nothing like that.' She paused. 'Shall I make some coffee?'

'That would be nice.' He stretched and, leaning back in his chair, linked his arms behind his head. There was something almost intimate about the gesture, as if he'd become completely relaxed in her company and totally at home.

Sophie fled to the kitchen. Why, oh, why did this have to be so difficult? she asked herself as she spooned fresh coffee into a cafetière. What was it about this man, Benedict, that seemed to have turned her world upside down since she'd met him? Was it just that he was so devastatingly good-looking? Or was it that he seemed exciting simply because technically he was out of bounds? Maybe, she told herself, if she hadn't already been in a relationship he wouldn't have been so appealing. But she knew that wouldn't have been the case even as the thought entered her head. Deep down she knew that Benedict would attract her whatever the circumstances.

Reaching up to one of the cupboards on the wall, she began taking down coffee-cups and saucers and it was then, as her arms were raised above her head, that once again, as before, she felt his arms go around her.

Unbeknown to her, he'd left the dining area and come quietly into the kitchen. It had felt good the last time it had happened and it felt good now. For one wild moment of abandon she leaned against him, content to be there, her head against his shoulder.

With his arms still tightly around her she felt his lips brush the nape of her neck. As a shaft of desire leapt inside her, and as he would have turned her to face him, suddenly reason returned and she began to struggle.

She sensed his surprise and when at last she succeeded in wriggling from his grasp and she turned to face him, it was confirmed in the expression in his eyes and in his raised eyebrows.

'Sophie...?' he said. 'What is it? What's wrong?'

'I'm sorry, Benedict,' she said. 'I can't.'

'But why? I don't understand.' He looked bewildered now. 'I thought...'

'I know. I know what you thought,' she said. 'And I'm sorry. Really, I am, but, you see, it's like this... I...I'm already in a relationship.'

She saw the hurt look in his eyes. Briefly it flared, then it was gone. His expression became inscrutable and it was impossible to gauge either his thoughts or his feelings.

'I see,' he said at last. 'Are you going to tell me about it?'

'Well...'

'Is it someone I know? Someone at the hospital maybe?'

'No. Nothing like that.' Suddenly her chest felt tight. 'He lives up north.' She turned away, unable to cope with being able to see him. With hands that trembled she busied herself with the coffee once more.

Benedict was silent until the coffee was ready. Sophie carried it on a tray into the sitting-room where she set it down on a low table, before perching herself on the edge of the sofa.

Only a few moments before he would probably have joined her on the sofa, sat beside her, perhaps put his arm around her, but now, because of that one short sentence, he sat at a distance, opposite her, in an armchair.

Desperately Sophie searched for something to say—something to break the silence that was growing between them and threatening to become unmanageable.

In the end it was Benedict who spoke. 'Is it serious,' he said, 'this relationship?'

'I thought it was,' Sophie replied carefully.

Benedict frowned. 'So has something happened to make you think otherwise?'

Sophie shrugged. 'I'm not sure. It's just that...I...I wonder whether it's actually going anywhere.' Leaning forward, she began to pour the coffee. Anything to avoid meeting his gaze and maybe having to face that look of hurt disappointment again.

'Want to tell me about it?' he asked, and when she didn't answer immediately he added, 'How did you meet?'

'At a medical conference.' Picking up his cup and saucer, she handed it to him.

'He's a doctor?'

'No,' she replied quickly. 'No, he's not a doctor, he's a rep for a pharmaceutical company. He came here to St Winifred's at the end of last year for a conference. We had lunch together, got talking and found that we got on rather well...'

'But you say he lives up north?'

'Yes, near Manchester, to be exact.'

'Do you get to see each other very often?'

'No, not really,' she admitted. 'He comes down when he can. He's coming next weekend, actually.'

'Will he stay for Christmas?'

Sophie shook her head. 'No, it's rather complicated. You see, he lives with his widowed father who's suffering from Parkinson's disease. He has help from Social Services when he's out on the road, but resources are limited at times like Christmas—besides, I've volunteered to work over Christmas anyway so there wouldn't be a lot of point in him coming here. We finally decided on next weekend so that Miles can come to the staff party with me.'

'I was going to ask you to come to that with me.' He spoke quietly but the disappointment was back in his eyes.

'Oh, Benedict. I'm sorry.' She stared at him in dismay.

'It's OK.' He shrugged. 'So is that his name—Miles?'

'Yes.' She nodded, aware of a feeling that could only really be described as misery beginning to creep over her. 'Miles Fraser.'

Benedict frowned.

'Do you know him?' asked Sophie quickly.

'No, I don't think so.'

'You frowned when you heard the name.'

'Just for a moment I thought I'd heard it somewhere before.'

'You may have done. After all, his work takes him to many hospitals. He knows Mr Crowley-Smith.'

'Really?' Benedict looked polite but far from interested.

'Yes, apparently Miles used to visit the hospital in Manchester where Mr Crowley-Smith was before he came to St Winifred's.'

'Well, I guess medical circles are pretty small but, no, I can't say I've heard of him.' Benedict paused. 'Do you get to go up to Manchester very often?'

Sophie shook her head. 'No, we agreed that it was best for Miles to come here because of his father. I don't think there's much room in the house and apparently the old gentleman gets very agitated if there's anyone else staying there.'

Benedict was silent for a moment then he drained his coffee-cup and stood up. 'Well,' he said, 'I guess I'd better be going.'

Sophie's heart sank. She'd felt sure he would have stayed longer if she hadn't told him about Miles. They would have talked on for hours about anything and everything, and now it was all ruined. 'You don't have to go,' she said in a small voice, looking up at him.

'Oh, but I think I do,' he said quietly, and she knew that with those few short words everything had now changed between them. 'If I stay we could both later regret it.'

She stood up and just for a moment they stood very close to one another, so close that she caught the scent of the cologne he was wearing. She looked up into his eyes and was further dismayed to see that the light of amusement, which she had come to know so well, was no longer there. It was gone, extinguished just like the candles on her table.

She swallowed and found that in spite of the coffee she'd recently drunk her throat was suddenly very dry. 'I hope…' she said, 'I hope we can still be friends, Benedict.'

He gave a tight little smile. Lifting his hand, he held the open palm against her cheek. It felt warm and comforting and she found herself inclining her head and pressing her face against it. 'I hope so, too,' he said at last. 'But I fear that may be difficult. You see, I'm not certain that with you, Sophie, I'd be able to simply settle for friendship.'

'Oh, Benedict, I'm so sorry. But I had to tell you.'

'Of course you did,' he said. 'It was just rather good there for a while to consider what might have been.' Withdrawing his hand, and speaking more briskly, he added, 'Thanks for the meal, Sophie. I'll see you on the ward.'

And then he was gone, out of her apartment and down the corridor to his own, leaving Sophie alone in the silence which suddenly was so claustrophobic it felt unbearable.

And that night when sleep proved to be a reluctant bedfellow, time and again she found her thoughts returning to Benedict's idea of considering what might have been if she'd been free and there had been no Miles.

The attraction between herself and Benedict had been instant. She knew that, just as she knew that, given free rein, it would very quickly have given way to the passion which had been smouldering beneath the surface. She'd felt it yesterday when she'd inadvertently found herself in his arms and they'd ended up kissing each other, and it had been there again tonight, throughout their meal and later when once again his arms had gone around her.

Who knew where it would have ended if she hadn't stopped him, if she hadn't told him about Miles? She could hardly believe it of herself that it could have progressed to full love-making on such a short acquaintance, but she was forced to admit that the intensity between them had suggested that had indeed been a possibility.

With a sigh she turned over again and stared at the ceiling, where a strip of light from the lamp outside in the courtyard was visible. What was wrong with her, for heaven's sake? Here she was in what had become a fairly long-term relationship, and even if she didn't see too much of Miles she shouldn't be allowing herself to get carried to such heights with a man she'd known so briefly.

The heartbreak of the situation was that deep down she knew she'd never felt for Miles quite what she was feeling for Benedict. This was something new and, if she was really honest, something she'd never felt for anyone else.

But she had to forget that now, put it right out of her mind. She'd made her decision, she'd told Benedict where he stood. All she could do now, she told herself firmly as she thumped her pillow for the umpteenth time, was to look forward to Miles's visit at the weekend.

So, if that was the case, why did she feel so miserable as the hours of that never-ending night ticked away?

CHAPTER NINE

'SOPHIE, you look terrible.'

'Thanks, Andrea.'

'Whatever's the matter?'

'Nothing really. I had a bad night, that's all.'

'Well, you'd better get yourself together before the weekend—parties and all that.' Andrea paused and once again peered suspiciously at Sophie. 'I take it you are coming to the staff party?'

'Oh, yes. Yes, of course,' Sophie replied.

'And Miles?' Andrea persisted. 'Is he still coming down?'

'As far as I know.' Sophie nodded then yawned. The two girls were in the sluice and had stopped for a chat, before returning to the hectic schedule of the ward.

'I'm still living in hopes that Benedict will ask me to go to the party with him.' Andrea gave a huge sigh. 'Honestly, I've thrown out enough hints, but he hardly seems to know that

I even exist. Perhaps I ought to get you to drop a few hints for me…'

'Me?' said Sophie in alarm. 'Why me?'

'Well, let's face it, you see more of him than any of us.'

'Oh, I don't know…'

'Well, you do. You must do. What with living with him.'

'Andrea! Would you mind rephrasing that, please?' Sophie protested. 'I most certainly do not live with him. We just happen to have apartments in the same block, that's all.'

'You know what I mean…you must *see* him.'

'Well, yes, but I'm not sure I could actually ask him that!'

'No?' Andrea said hopefully, then added with a sigh, 'I guess not. Oh, well, never mind. Maybe I'll just have to pluck up courage myself…'

With that Andrea bustled away back onto the ward, leaving Sophie with her thoughts in turmoil. She had no idea what her friend would have thought if she'd told her what had happened the night before. Whatever would Andrea's reaction have been if she'd said that

Benedict had actually been about to ask her, Sophie, to the staff party?

Maybe she should put in a word for Andrea, even though her every instinct told her that she didn't think she could bring herself to do such a thing.

She stood for a moment, deliberating. It was nearly time for the doctors' daily round and she was dreading seeing Benedict again after the previous evening. There had been no sign of him that morning when she'd left for work, and when she'd reached the hospital she'd seen his car already parked in the staff car park.

It was, however, one of those frantically busy mornings, with three admissions, one discharge and a theatre list, and Sophie knew that by lingering in the sluice she was wasting precious time. In a conscious effort to pull herself together, she gave herself a little shake and smoothed down the skirt of her uniform then, taking a deep breath, she walked briskly back onto the ward.

A quick glance around showed her that the new admissions had started to arrive so, after checking on Nathan and finding him listening to his music and thumping his locker in time to the rhythm of the *Radetzky March*, she made her way to the nurses' station.

'Ah, Nurse Quentin...' Sister Bailey raised her eyebrows as Sophie approached. 'There you are. I was about to send out a search party.'

'No need for that, Sister,' Sophie replied crisply. 'I'm here now.'

'Yes, well.' Sister looked faintly surprised at Sophie's uncharacteristic retort. 'I want you to do William Davis's admission—he's coming to us instead of to the day unit for his tonsillectomy. His consultant wants tests run on him because of a series of reccurent infections. Now, this is William.' She turned to a rather large boy with cropped hair who was accompanied by a short, thickset man dressed in working overalls.

'Hello, William.' Sophie gave a bright smile that drew no response whatsoever from the boy. 'Hello, Mr Davis—I'm Staff Nurse Sophie Quentin.'

'Name's Armstrong,' said the man with a grunt, 'not Davis.'

'Oh, I'm sorry, I assumed...'

'His mother's name's Davis—we ain't married.'

'Oh, I see. Right, well, if you'd both like to come with me, we have some forms to fill in.'

'Take long, will it?' muttered the man. 'I have to get to work. I'm late as it is. I thought I'd only have to drop him off.'

'You're not staying with William, then?' asked Sophie as she ushered them into an empty interview room.

'Stayin'? Course I'm not stayin'. What would I want to stay for? It's him what's havin' his tonsils out, not me.' The man made a noise which Sophie presumed was meant to be a laugh.

'I see.' Sophie smiled at William but still there was no response. 'So, what about William's mother?'

'What about her?'

'Will she be coming in?'

'Yeah, later. She's seein' to the other kids at the moment.'

'Right. Well, I need you to answer some questions for me, Mr…er Mr Armstrong.'

'What sorta questions?'

'Well, firstly, if I could just check that William is William Mark Davis.'

'Of course he is. Who do you think he is?'

'And that his date of birth is 6 April 1991.'

'I dunno. Is that your birthday?' Mr Armstrong turned blankly to the boy.

William nodded.

Sophie moved on to his address which, fortunately, Mr Armstrong did seem to know. 'Now,' she said, 'who is your GP?'

'Oh, for pity's sake!' Mr Armstrong was growing red in the face. 'How many more of these bloody stupid questions? *I* don't know. My doctor is Jenkins but his mother's with another one and I presume she's got the kids with him, too.'

'It's Dr Frampton,' said William suddenly, speaking for the first time.

'Thank you, William,' said Sophie quietly. 'The next thing I need to know is whether you've had any operations before.' William shook his head. 'What about illnesses?' Sophie looked at Mr Armstrong.

'Haven't got a clue. You had chickenpox, didn't you?'

William nodded.

'And mumps.'

'No, I didn't have mumps—that was our Edward.'

'You did have mumps. I remember 'cos yer mother said I had to keep away from you.'

'No, that was Eddie,' said William.

'Don't worry,' Sophie intervened when it looked as if it might be about to escalate into a full-scale argument between them. 'I'll check with William's mother later. Now, what about religion?'

'What about it?' Mr Armstrong looked as if he might be about to explode. 'Look, I told you, I'm in a hurry. I can't sit here any longer, listening to all this rubbish.'

'All right,' said Sophie, writing 'C of E' in the religion slot, together with a question mark. 'Well, I think that's just about all anyway, Mr Armstrong. I shall be showing William to his bed now. Would you like to come with us before you go and perhaps help him unpack?'

'I'm sure he's quite capable of unpackin' his own bag—great lad like him. I'll get along now. You make sure you behave yourself, William. D'you hear me? I don't want no reports from these nurses that you've been up to any of your old tricks—if I do, you know what to expect. Don't you?'

'Yes.' William stared at his feet.

'See you, then.'

'Just a moment, Mr Armstrong—we need you to sign the consent form,' said Sophie quickly, as Mr Armstrong stood up and moved towards the door.

'He's not having the operation till tomorrow, is he?'

'No…'

'In that case, his mother can sign it when she comes in later.'

With that he was gone, leaving Sophie and William looking at each other.

'Well, William,' said Sophie at last with a sigh, 'I guess we'd better go and unpack your bag…' She paused, looking around. 'You do have a bag?'

'I got some things in here.' The boy held up a supermarket carrier bag.

'Come on, then,' said Sophie gently as she recognised a flicker of fear in the boy's eyes as he realised he was alone in this strange place. 'I'll show you where you're going to sleep.'

As they walked out of the office onto the ward the first person they saw was Jefferson, who was struggling under the weight of a large Christmas tree. 'Oh, wonderful,' cried Sophie. 'Is that for us?'

'Well, I hope it is,' said Jefferson, stopping to wipe his brow. ''Cos if it isn't I'll have to get it all back downstairs again.'

Sophie laughed. Looking down at William, she said, 'You'll be able to help decorate it later, won't you, William?'

The boy didn't answer but Sophie was pleased to see that he looked a bit happier as he walked beside her down the ward. As they passed Antonia's bed Sophie noticed that the girl was asleep, while her brother Sean and her sister Fleur sat on either side of her bed. Sean was engrossed in a book and Fleur had swivelled round in her chair in order to watch another video that Tom was engrossed in. This time it appeared to feature dolphins and Sophie saw William's look of interest as they passed.

When they reached his bed she opened his locker. 'You can keep your things in here, William,' she said. 'I'd like you to get undressed in a moment and put on your pyjamas because I need to do a few jobs, like taking your temperature.' She paused and swung the locker round, revealing a rail and a soap dish on the back. 'You can put your towel on here,' she said, indicating the rail, 'and that little dish is for your soap.'

The boy looked blank and she looked at the carrier bag he still clutched tightly in one hand. 'You do have wash things with you, don't you, William?'

He shook his head.

'Never mind,' she said hastily. 'I'll get some things for you. Maybe you'd like to get undressed while I'm gone.' She began to draw the curtains while William sat in silence on the bed.

In the treatment room Sophie found soap, facecloth, toothbrush and toothpaste, towel and a comb in the supplies which were kept there for just such a situation. When she returned to the bed it was to find that William hadn't moved.

'William...?' she said. When he looked up, she went on, 'I thought you were going to get into your pyjamas.'

The boy put his head down and mumbled something. Sophie bent down. 'Sorry, William, what did you say?' she asked gently.

'Haven't got no pyjamas,' he muttered.

'Oh, I see. Well, never mind. Maybe we can find you a spare pair…'

'Got these.' He opened his carrier bag and pulled out a grubby T-shirt and a pair of boxer shorts. There was something else in the bag but he screwed it up again quickly so that Sophie couldn't see what it was.

'Well, that's fine,' she said. 'You get changed and I'll be back in a few minutes.'

Outside in the ward Sophie closed her eyes and took a deep breath to steady herself. A few seconds later, when she opened her eyes again, she realised that the doctors' round had started and they were grouped around Nathan who had apparently had enough of his music and had decided it was high time he made his presence known again.

Benedict was with them. Of course he was. She'd known he would be there, but that knowledge did nothing to stop the painful twisting of her heart as this morning, for the

first time since he'd joined Paediatrics, he
didn't allow his eyes to meet hers.

But why should he? Why would he? It had
all changed now, she told herself miserably as,
with her head down, she hurried back to the
nurses' station. Before, they had both been
only too aware of an attraction between them,
a kind of magic that said that the chemistry
was right. But that awareness had gone now
ever since she'd told him about Miles. Maybe
it was her own fault for even acknowledging
that awareness in the first place when she'd
known only too well that she wasn't free to do
so.

At the nurses' station she collected an ear-
probe and a sphygmomanometer in order to
check William's temperature and blood pressure. On the way back to his bed, on a sudden
impulse, as she passed the play area she picked
up a few books that she thought might appeal
to him.

By the time she reached William's bed the
doctors were grouped around Antonia. Sophie
saw that Sean and Fleur were no longer there,
no doubt having gone to the relatives' rest
room, and that Antonia was now awake and

smiling weakly at something Benedict had said.

William had changed into his boxer shorts and T-shirt, which Sophie could see had a Batman motif on the front. He was bundling his clothes into his locker, together with the carrier bag which now appeared to be empty.

'William,' she said as she drew back the curtains, 'the doctors are just coming...'

'What for?' The fear was back in his eyes.

'It's all right. They probably only want to say hello.'

'They won't stick needles in me, will they?'

'No, of course not.'

'My brother said they would.'

'I promise there won't be any needles to-day,' said Sophie firmly.

'There will be tomorrow, though, won't there?' The boy's eyes darkened.

'Yes,' Sophie replied truthfully. 'There probably will be. But I promise, if there are, I will do them and I'm the best needle-sticker-inner on the ward. You ask Tom. Isn't that right, Tom?' she called across to the next bed.

'What?' Tom turned from the television where the credits were beginning to roll, signifying the end of the film.

'I was just telling William here that I'm the best one to give injections. Isn't that so?'

'Yes,' Tom replied solemnly. 'She is. She doesn't hurt at all.'

'Good morning, Staff Nurse Quentin. Who do we have here?'

Sophie turned and found the doctors grouped behind her. 'Good morning, Mr Crowley-Smith,' she replied. 'This is William Davis. He's here for a tonsillectomy tomorrow. So he's on the ENT list for Mr Collingwood.'

'Yes, yes, quite. Well, young man, welcome to the children's ward,' said Mr Crowley-Smith. 'Your doctor will be along to see you in due course.' He moved away, leaving Sophie to carry out William's preliminary observations. Still she hadn't caught Benedict's eye, and as he, too, moved down the ward with the rest of Mr Crowley-Smith's entourage her heart felt heavier than ever.

When William's tests were completed Sophie gave him the books she'd brought from the play area. 'I don't know what you like,' she said, 'and if you don't fancy these there are plenty more. You don't have to stay in bed today.' As she spoke, she leaned across the bed to straighten the covers, and as she did so she caught sight of a very worn, slightly battered teddy bear which had been tucked beneath the covers. Guessing that this had been what William had tried to conceal in his plastic carrier bag, she pretended not to see it.

'D'you want to watch my dolphin video?' asked Tom suddenly.

'Don't mind,' said William with a shrug.

'Come on,' said Tom. 'Come and sit over here and I'll wind it back.'

William glanced at Sophie and when she nodded and smiled he moved round his bed and sat in the chair beside Tom.

Sophie made her way back to the nurses' station, where she found Andrea.

'What's up?' asked Andrea.

'What do you mean?' Sophie frowned.

'Well, it was bad enough when you just looked tired—you look fierce now as well.'

'I've just admitted young William Davis.' Sophie spoke quietly so that no one else could overhear.

'Problems?' asked Andrea.

'I could have wept,' said Sophie, shaking her head.

'That bad?'

'He had next to nothing with him—no pyjamas, no wash gear, no dressing-gown or slippers. Just a carrier bag with a T-shirt and boxer shorts and his teddy. And as if that wasn't enough, his mother's partner didn't even stay to see him installed. Honestly, Andrea, I try not to let these situations get to me, but sometimes... I don't know...' Sophie swallowed hard and trailed off.

'I know,' said Andrea. 'Sometimes it gets you right here, doesn't it?' She thumped her heart as she spoke. 'And we seem to be having more than our fair share at the moment as well. What with Antonia...and Tom...'

'It's if there are signs of neglect or when I think they might be going short on love that it gets to me,' said Sophie.

'Well, there's no shortage of love over there.' Andrea inclined her head in the direction of Antonia's bed.

Sophie looked up and saw that Sean and Fleur had returned and had been joined by their mother who never seemed to be far from her elder daughter's side. 'They seem to be coping well…so far,' she said.

'It's getting depressing in here,' said Andrea, taking a deep breath. 'I suggest that as soon as we get the chance we start decorating the tree.'

'Good idea.' Sophie nodded, brightening up a little at the thought. 'William will be able to help with that.'

There wasn't a lull until nearly the end of Sophie's and Andrea's shift, but both girls agreed they would stay on to help Jefferson and Sister Bailey with the decorating of the ward. Even Benedict and Samir turned up to lend a hand, and in the end practically everyone joined in, even Sean and Fleur, while Antonia watched breathlessly, her eyes shining, her hands clasped tightly together as one by one the glittering baubles were suspended from the branches of the tree.

Sophie managed to involve both William and Tom, who helped by passing her paperchains, and balloons, and plastic angels with glittering wings which she used to decorate the shelves around the ward.

'I've never had a Christmas tree before,' said William as he turned and gazed up at the laden tree.

'My dad said he was going to get one for me and Sara,' said Tom.

'We always have a tree,' said Fleur. 'But usually Antonia helps me to decorate it. She's really good at decorating Christmas trees.'

'Well, it's a good job we've got Antonia here to help us with this one, isn't it?' said Benedict from the top of the stepladder. 'Where do you want these bows, Antonia?' he called down to the child in the bed.

'Over there,' Antonia replied happily. 'On that branch... No, not that one, the one below... Yes, that's right.'

It was a happy time for children and staff alike, but Sophie was still aware of an ache somewhere in her heart that simply wouldn't go away.

And it went on throughout the day, in spite of her efforts to ignore it. Any spare time she had was spent unpacking and settling into her apartment or wrapping Christmas gifts as she endeavoured to keep busy in the belief that it was the only way to make the situation with Benedict go away.

The following day William went to Theatre for his tonsillectomy, and Sophie was relieved when his mother arrived before the operation and stayed with her son for several hours afterwards.

'I don't think she dared do otherwise,' said Andrea darkly, 'not after her session in the office. Sister took a very dim view of her casual attitude towards William.'

Tom's father also arrived after lunch and spent a long session in the office with Sister Bailey, Benedict, Rosemary and the duty social worker, where it was agreed that Tom could go home for Christmas Day and Boxing Day, returning to the ward to continue his treatment on the following day.

'I was afraid it would be too traumatic for him, going to the house where the attack took place,' Sophie commented to Andrea while they were discussing the situation before going off duty, 'but Sister said they're going to stay with his father's parents at their home.'

'What about Tom's little sister?'

'Yes, apparently she's going, too.'

'It looks as if there could be a happy ending after all to that dreadful affair.'

Sophie nodded. 'Yes, provided the mother pulls through. Apparently she's still far from well.'

Just before she went off duty Sophie went to have another look at William, who was once again on his own as his mother had just left the ward. Sophie hadn't been able to take to William's mother who seemed to have spent most of her time at the hospital outside in the corridor, smoking one cigarette after another.

He was still sleepy from the after-effects of the anaesthetic and was huddled under the covers when Sophie reached his bed. 'Hello, William.' She bent over him and felt his forehead. 'How are you feeling?'

'My throat hurts.' His voice was little more than a harsh whisper.

'It's bound to hurt for a time,' Sophie replied.

'My doctor said my throat wouldn't be so bad if I had my tonsils out,' whispered William, pulling a face. 'This is worse than it's ever been.'

'It will get better, William,' said Sophie. 'But one of the good things about having your tonsils out is that you get to have lots of ice cream.'

'I don't want any ice cream,' said William. 'I don't want nothing.' Turning his face to the wall, he pulled the cover up around his ears.

'You *will* feel better tomorrow, William,' said Sophie. 'I promise.'

She didn't see Benedict again that day and it was late when she finally left the hospital. It was another crisply cold day, and as the afternoon light faded there was more than a hint of the frost that would soon descend.

When Sophie reached the car park she glanced back at the children's ward and in the window she could see the twinkling lights of the tree they'd decorated the day before. There was so much human drama being played out at the present time in that one room that she found herself praying that all those situations could be suspended, put on hold in some way until after the festivities. Her training as a nurse, however, had taught her otherwise—life simply wasn't like that. People would go on getting hurt or falling ill or destroying each other either physically or emotionally no matter what time of year it was.

With a little shiver Sophie turned away. Pulling up her coat collar before unlocking her car, she glanced across to where Benedict usually parked his car. The space was empty, which meant he'd already left.

The empty space seemed to Sophie somehow synonymous with the emptiness she'd felt inside since that moment when Benedict had left her apartment.

The festive air in the town as she drove through it was in complete contrast to her mood, with a Father Christmas in the square beside the Christmas tree, stamping his feet to keep out the cold, hundreds of twinkling fairy lights strung between the lamp posts, and around the window of the butcher's shop in the high street dozens of hapless turkeys.

By the time Sophie reached Clifton Court the blinds in Benedict's apartment were drawn. Disconsolately, she trailed up the stairs to her own apartment. If the truth were known, she would have given anything to tap on his door in passing, to stop for a chat and maybe a drink, but it seemed that now that Benedict knew about Miles such gestures of neighbourliness had not only changed but might never be possible again. She simply had to get used to it, she told herself miserably as she let herself into her own apartment.

Her phone started ringing even before she'd taken her coat off, and for one wild moment she thought it might be Benedict. Maybe he'd seen her arrive home. Maybe after all he'd come to the conclusion that they could still be friends.

Slipping out of her coat, she tossed it, together with her bag and her keys, onto the sofa. Perhaps he was going to ask her in for that drink after all.

By the time she'd grabbed the receiver her heart was thumping and she'd so convinced herself that it was Benedict on the other end of the line that it came as a real shock to hear Miles's voice.

CHAPTER TEN

'OH,' SOPHIE said. 'Miles, it's you.'

'Yes, it's me. Were you expecting somebody else?'

'Er, no. Not exactly. It's just that I'm surprised you're phoning this early. I thought you might phone later, this evening, maybe...' Sophie trailed off, aware of the fact that she was waffling.

'No,' he said, 'I didn't think I should leave it until this evening.'

'Why? What is it? What's wrong?'

'Well...'

It was as far as he got for Sophie intervened. 'You're not coming down tomorrow, are you?'

'No, my love, I'm afraid not.'

She should have been upset, angry even, or at the very least disappointed, but she was none of these things. Her first reaction was almost one of relief because now she could go to the staff party with Benedict.

The thought, utterly outrageous as it was, she dismissed the instant it entered her mind. Of course she couldn't go with Benedict. Just because Miles wasn't coming down for this one weekend, it didn't change anything. Wearily she heard herself say, 'What is it this time? Your father again?'

'Don't say it like that.' He sounded hurt, affronted even. 'Yes, it is Dad again, as it happens, but he can't help it Sophie. It isn't his fault, any more than it's my fault. As it is, he's had a bad turn. He's spent the last forty-eight hours in hospital.'

'Oh, Miles, I'm sorry. Really I am.' Suddenly she felt dreadful for what she'd said and even worse over what she'd thought. 'Is he home now?'

'Yes, he is,' Miles replied stiffly, 'but I can hardly just go off and leave him to fend for himself—can I?'

'No,' she replied quickly. 'No, of course you can't.'

There was a long silence then Miles spoke again. 'I feel awful about this as well. I won't even be able to give you your Christmas present now. But, listen, I think I've managed to work something out.'

'Oh, really?' She tried to sound enthusiastic but inside she felt nothing.

'Yes, I have to come south during the second week in January for the firm. I've already arranged for Dad to go into a residential respite care home and I've been thinking—if you could get some time off work maybe I could extend that stay by a few days. I thought perhaps we could go down into Devon or Cornwall.'

'In January?' said Sophie faintly.

'We could find a nice country hotel—you know, log fires and oak beams, that sort of thing...'

'Hmm.' She sounded far from convinced.

'You're angry with me, aren't you, Sophie?' he said accusingly.

'I don't know that I'm angry. It's just that... Oh, I don't know, it's Christmas. We were going to the staff party together, and I wanted you to see my new flat...'

'And I will,' he said firmly. 'We just have to be patient. I am sorry, darling. Please, don't be angry with me. I promise I'll make it up to you soon.'

They talked for a further ten minutes or so, then, with further promises on Miles's part that he would ring again on Christmas Eve, they hung up.

Afterwards Sophie felt even more flat than she had before. She knew that Miles couldn't help the fact that his father was so ill, just as she knew he couldn't just walk away and leave him whenever the fancy took him, but that still did little to ease the frustration she felt when time after time their plans would have to be changed or abandoned, sometimes at a moment's notice.

Briefly she wondered whether she would even bother going to the staff party now that Miles wouldn't be with her, but then she decided that would be silly—she had enough friends at work to guarantee that she would have a good time even if she did go unaccompanied.

The following day Sophie was off duty. She had deliberately planned it that way in the hope that Miles might have been able to come down early then they could have spent some time together before the party. As it was, she spent part of the day shopping and was on the point of going to see her mother when she thought better of it and went home instead.

Her mother would be sure to ask about Miles, and when Sophie told her he wasn't coming down it would, no doubt, raise further speculation on her mother's part. This in turn would lead to yet more speculation about the fact that Sophie would now be going to the staff party on her own—and would that nice Mr Lawrence be there? Sophie had instinctively always known that her mother didn't really like Miles and somehow she felt she simply couldn't cope with her at the moment.

If the truth were known, she was having enough trouble with her own feelings and emotions, without having anyone else adding fuel to the fire.

She'd bought a new dress for the party, and after she'd trailed home from the shops and dumped her shopping on the kitchen floor, she wandered into her bedroom and took it out of the wardrobe. It was black satin with a short skirt and very thin shoulder straps onto which had been sewn dozens of tiny emerald-coloured glass stones that glittered every time they caught the light.

Antonia had asked her what she was going to wear and had sat on her bed, listening enthralled as Sophie had described her dress. 'And your shoes?' she'd asked when Sophie had finished. 'Have you got new shoes as well?'

'No.' Sophie had laughed. 'My strappy high heels from last year will have to do.'

'How high are they?' Antonia had breathed, then had gasped as Sophie had indicated the height between finger and thumb. 'I wish I could have shoes with heels,' she'd said wistfully, 'but Mummy won't let me.'

Sophie had been about to say that no doubt she could when she was older, then she'd remembered and had bitten her lip. Maybe, she thought now as she took her own shoes from the wardrobe floor and inspected them, she should just have said it anyway and allowed Antonia the pleasure of anticipation.

She took a long time getting ready. She soaked for an hour in the softly scented water of a foam bath, after washing her hair, and later she found herself taking extra care over her nails and her make-up, before stepping into her dress. When she was ready she gazed critically at herself in the mirror. The dress looked good and her hair shone like spun gold.

Throughout the time she'd spent getting ready, she'd been aware of a steadily mounting sense of excitement, which had had an added edge of guilt to it because, deep down, she'd known that because Miles wasn't going to be there she should have been feeling no such thing.

When she finally let herself out of her apartment it was to find that the rest of the complex was silent. She'd hardly seen any of her neighbours since she'd moved in, and as she hurried along the softly lit corridor to the lift, her heels making no sound on the thick carpet, she found herself wondering just who were behind some of those firmly closed doors and what they were doing. Were they getting ready for Christmas parties or other festivities, or were they pursuing more simple pleasures, like reading or watching television?

There was only silence from behind Benedict's door and Sophie wondered if he'd already left. She almost knocked to ask if he'd like a lift, but even as she hesitated her courage deserted her and she hurried on.

The hospital was a blaze of lights like a beacon as Sophie drove out of the town and up the hill. Circling the building, she parked at the rear in the car park of the social club.

There were three staff parties being held in the build-up to Christmas, each on separate nights with lots being drawn as to who should attend which one and who should be on duty.

The car park was nearly full, and as Sophie locked her car and pulled her wrap around her she could hear the steady thump of the music from the club. She glanced around but couldn't see Benedict's car anywhere, which suggested he might still have been in his flat when she'd left Clifton Court. Crossing the car park, she pushed open the glass door and was met by a rush of warm air and a loud blast of music.

'Hello, Sophie.' Jefferson was in the foyer. Dressed in a dazzling white shirt, black trousers and a burgundy-coloured jacket in crushed velvet, his skin shone like ebony.

She smiled. 'Hello, Jefferson. Do you know if Andrea is here yet?'

'Yes, I think I saw her just now.' A frown crossed his face, replacing his huge smile. 'You're not on your own?' he asked in concern.

'Yes, Jefferson, I suppose I am.' She laughed. 'On the other hand, I guess you can't really be alone in a crowd like ours.' She paused and eyed him up and down. 'Are you on door duty?'

He nodded. 'Yes, I am, but if I'd known you were coming on your own I would never have volunteered.'

Sophie laughed up at him as he towered above her. 'Never mind,' she said. 'I must say you certainly look the part.'

'I won't be out here all night,' he said. 'Would you let me buy you a drink later on…and maybe have a dance…?'

'Of course, Jefferson. Thank you. I'll look forward to it,' Sophie replied.

After leaving her coat in the cloakroom, Sophie took a deep breath and prepared to join the fray. The lights were dim inside the club and the DJ was playing vintage Christmas hits from years gone by which everyone knew. Hardly anyone was dancing. Most people were congregated around the bar or seated at tables in the alcoves that surrounded the dance floor.

She stood for a moment inside the doors, trying to get her eyes accustomed to the light while she looked around to see who had arrived. She knew most people, although some only slightly or by sight. What she was really looking for were some of the paediatric staff with whom she could sit.

Then from the other side of the room she caught sight of someone waving frantically and trying to attract her attention. Narrowing her eyes slightly and peering into the gloom, she realised it was Andrea.

'Yoohoo, Sophie! Come on, we're over here. We've saved places for you.'

She made her way across the room, waving and acknowledging one or two others who called out to her as she passed.

'Thank goodness you've got here,' cried Andrea as she reached the table. 'I was having the devil of a job, trying to save places. People keep wanting to join us.'

'Us?' Sophie looked round at the empty seats around the table. 'Who are ''us''?'

'Well, there's Cheryl—she's gone to the loo—and there's Samir and…' She paused, her face shining with suppressed excitement. 'You'll never guess what I did,' she added, suddenly grabbing Sophie's arm.

'No, I never will, Andrea, not with you,' said Sophie with a laugh as she sat down. 'But I'm sure you're going to tell me anyway.'

'I asked him,' said Andrea with a look of triumph on her face.

'You asked who what?' said Sophie blankly.

'I asked Benedict if he was going to the party.'

Sophie felt herself stiffen at mention of Benedict's name. 'Oh?' she said casually. 'And what did he say?'

'He said, yes, he was going, so then I asked him if he had anyone to go with. When he said no, I decided to go for it. I told him I didn't have anyone to go with either, and why didn't we go together?'

'What did he say?' For some reason Sophie suddenly felt as if she might be about to suffocate.

'He said, ''Fine, why not?'' Honestly, Sophie, I can hardly believe it. I don't even think he'd noticed me before, and now here I am with him as my date. Isn't it amazing?'

'Yes, amazing,' said Sophie faintly. Looking round, she said, 'So where is he?'

''He's up at the bar, getting drinks with Samir...' She paused again and peered at Sophie. 'Is that where yours is?'

'Sorry?' Sophie frowned.

'Your Miles. I'm dying to meet him—so is Cheryl. She says if you're prepared to ignore any attention from Benedict because of him, this Miles must be pretty impressive.'

'What does she mean—ignore attention from Benedict?' demanded Sophie.

'Don't pretend you don't know,' scoffed Andrea. 'Everyone on the unit has noticed the way he's been looking at you. None of the rest of us stood a chance with him until you told him about Miles. Come on, which one is Miles?' She craned her neck and peered at the men at the bar. 'Is it that blond guy over there?'

'No,' Sophie replied quietly. 'It isn't. Miles isn't here, Andrea.'

'What? Hasn't he come down?'

Sophie shook her head. 'No, he couldn't get away.'

'Not his father again!'

'Yes. Apparently he took a turn for the worse.'

'Isn't that excuse wearing a bit thin?' said Andrea.

'What do you mean?' Sophie tried to sound indignant but feared somehow it wasn't having the desired effect.

Andrea shrugged, declining to comment any further, and as at that precise moment the men returned to the table with drinks Sophie had something other than Miles and his excuses to think about.

Benedict looked even more handsome than usual in a pale grey silk shirt and black trousers. He must have already seen her as he crossed the floor because when she looked up her eyes immediately met his. He allowed his gaze to sweep over her, before setting the drinks down on the table. At the same moment Cheryl returned to the table and demanded to know where Miles was, and Sophie found herself explaining not only to Cheryl but also to Benedict and Samir why she was alone.

'This is no problem,' said Samir. 'Join us. I get you a drink.'

'Oh, no, really…' Sophie began.

'I insist,' said Samir. 'It's my round.'

'Very well. Thank you. I'll have an orange juice.'

'Oh, have something a bit stronger than that,' said Cheryl. 'This is a party, for goodness' sake.'

'I'm driving—' Sophie began.

'You can share my taxi,' said Cheryl. 'Leave your car here. You can always pick it up in the morning.'

'Oh, all right, then,' said Sophie. 'In that case, I'll have a glass of wine.'

She found it hard to relax in spite of the wine. Benedict was simply too close for comfort, and later, seeing him dance a slow, smoochy number with Andrea, she was struck by a wave of emotion so strong that it threatened to engulf her. She was unfamiliar with jealousy but surely this is what this is, she thought as miserably she watched the pair of them on the dance floor.

Andrea had her arms around Benedict's neck, with her head resting on his shoulder, while Benedict was holding her close, both hands resting on the small of her back.

Sophie looked away, biting her lip, and then, startled, she glanced up as she realised someone had spoken to her. She found Samir leaning across the table, an anxious expression on his face. 'Oh, I'm sorry, Samir,' she said. 'I was miles away. What did you say?'

'I ask you to dance,' he said, his dark, expressive eyes suddenly disconcertingly knowing.

'Of course.' She rose to her feet, took his outstretched hand and allowed him to lead her onto the dance floor.

'You are unhappy, Sophie,' he said as he drew her into his arms.

'Oh, dear.' Sophie pulled a face. 'Is it that obvious?'

'There would be those who would say it is understandable—your unhappiness—if your man breaks a promise to you. But me, I think there is more to your unhappiness than that.'

'I don't know what you mean, Samir,' Sophie replied. As she moved round, over Samir's shoulder she could see Benedict's face above the tumble of Andrea's auburn hair.

'Oh, but I think you do.' Leaning back slightly and holding her away from him, he glanced across at Benedict and Andrea. 'Back home in Romania, my mother, she say, ''Be true to yourself.'' She always say that.'

'If only it were that simple,' said Sophie.

'Usually it is,' Samir replied. 'Because if you not true to yourself, there is no point in anything because someday you pay a high price.'

As he spoke Samir moved her round again so that Benedict was out of Sophie's vision, but not before, for the briefest of moments, Benedict's eyes had met hers, and deep inside she'd once again felt that awful pang of anguish at seeing another woman in his arms.

The evening went on and the pre-Christmas fun grew fast and furious with a buffet supper followed by games and more dancing. Jefferson came and claimed his dance from Sophie then bought a drink, not only for her but also for Cheryl with whom he spent the rest of the evening.

Sophie had just reached the point where she was wishing it could all be over so that she could go home and find some peace to try to unravel her tangled emotions, but as she was returning from a trip to the cloakroom and was about to sit down she felt a hand on her arm. Turning quickly, she found Benedict at her side and her heart leapt crazily against her ribs.

'My turn, I think,' he murmured, drawing her onto a floor strewn with party streamers and helium-filled balloons that bobbed about or drifted to the ceiling. The DJ had gone through all the predictable Christmas hits, from Slade to Bing Crosby, and had now resorted to the dreamy, late night sort of music associated with lovers.

As his arms went around her she melted to his touch, and as Celine Dion told someone that her heart would go on Sophie gave herself up to the brief but sure ecstasy of being in Benedict's arms once more.

'So you're alone again?' he said softly, his mouth against her ear.

She nodded. 'It was unavoidable,' she replied.

'I see.' He sounded far from convinced and she threw him a sharp glance.

'If you were my girl I wouldn't let you out of my sight, looking the way you do tonight, never mind having you come alone to a party full of randy doctors.'

'Do you include yourself in that?' she asked lightly, only too aware of the admiration in his eyes.

'What do you think?' he murmured.

'You've been cool with me the last few days,' she said after a while, her tone faintly accusing.

'Put it down to disappointment,' he replied with a slight shrug.

'You seem to have got over it now.' She allowed her glance to turn to Andrea who was dancing with Samir.

'She was very insistent,' he said, following her gaze. 'But I have to say I was pleasantly surprised. She's excellent company.' He paused then, changing the subject, said, 'So, does this mean you don't get to see your... friend at all over Christmas?'

She shook her head, unable to speak, still fighting the new sharp stab of jealousy at Benedict being surprised by Andrea and finding her to be excellent company.

'That must be tough. I always think Christmas is a time for lovers to be together.'

She didn't answer—couldn't—because of the lump in her throat. Instead, she simply held on to him a little tighter.

All too soon it was over and he was leading her back to their table where he was immediately claimed by Andrea once again. It was getting late by this time and the crowd in the club had started to thin out. While Benedict and Andrea were still on the floor, Cheryl went out to the foyer, only to return immediately to say that her cab had arrived.

There was no time for goodbyes as Sophie followed Cheryl outside and, after much giggling and a lingering goodnight between Cheryl and Jefferson, the two girls climbed into the taxi.

'D'you know, he's really nice is Jefferson,' sighed Cheryl as she collapsed into the back seat beside Sophie. 'I don't know why I never noticed before.' She giggled, clearly slightly tipsy from the vodkas she'd drunk during the course of the evening. 'He said he's going to ring me. Pity he couldn't come home with us. He could have come in for coffee.'

'I wonder how the others are getting home,' murmured Sophie.

'Oh, they'll have a cab—at least, they came in a cab so I imagine they'll go home in one as well.' Cheryl giggled helplessly again. 'Andrea seemed to be getting on very well with our Dr Lawrence, didn't she? I bet *he* gets asked in for coffee when they get to her place.'

Sophie didn't answer, instead turning her head and staring out of the window at the dark, deserted streets. She didn't want to think about Benedict being invited in for coffee. In fact, it was the last thing she wanted to think about. She was vaguely aware of Cheryl prattling away by her side but she took little further notice of what she was saying. It had been a strange evening, leaving Sophie with mixed feelings. She wasn't even sure whether she was glad she had gone or not…

'And it seems such a shame. Poor old Samir, and there's Andrea who hardly knows he exists. She's only got eyes for Benedict—'

'What did you say?' Sophie, suddenly aware of what Cheryl was saying, turned her head.

'What?' Cheryl turned to look at her but even in the half-light inside the cab her eyes looked glazed.

'About Samir. You said something about Samir.'

'Did I?' Cheryl giggled again.

'Yes, you said poor old Samir, and then something about Andrea,' said Sophie impatiently.

'Oh, that. Well he's nuts about her, isn't he?'

'Is he?' Sophie frowned in the darkness. 'I didn't know that.'

'I thought you were her friend.'

'Well, yes, I am,' Sophie admitted. 'But I didn't know that. She's never said anything about him.'

'It's like I said—she hardly knows he's there.'

'How do you know this?'

'Staffroom gossip. I heard it from that occupational therapist—I can't remember her name, the one with the dreadlocks.'

'Jessica Redfern.'

'That's the one, and she heard it from one of the housemen who'd got it from Samir himself. But, like I say, it hasn't done him a lot of good because Andrea's all gooey-eyed over Benedict. He didn't seem to know *she* existed until tonight, 'cos he was too busy drooling over you—but after what I saw on the dance floor, well, it's anybody's guess where they'll end up tonight.'

Sophie swallowed and once again turned miserably away.

'Shame about your bloke,' said Cheryl after a while. 'Him not getting down and all that.'

'Yes.' Sophie nodded. 'Yes, it was.' Once again she turned her face away to gaze with unseeing eyes out of the window.

Her heart felt like lead as the taxi hurtled on through the night, taking her back to the loneliness of her apartment. But when they reached Clifton Court and she paid Cheryl her share of the fare she wondered what the other girl would make of it if she knew that her misery had nothing to do with the fact that Miles hadn't been able to come down.

CHAPTER ELEVEN

SOPHIE couldn't sleep. It was impossible because all she could see in her mind's eye was an image of Benedict and Andrea together. They would have gone to Andrea's flat in their taxi and, as Cheryl had said, Andrea would have been sure to have asked him in for coffee. Once inside, well, it didn't need too much imagination to know how their evening would have ended.

Turning her head, she looked at her bedside clock. The hands stood at three o'clock. Was he still there? Were they even now in bed together? Was he making love to Andrea? Switching on her bedside light, Sophie sat up. She could bear this torture no longer.

Slipping from her bed, she padded to the kitchen where she made herself a hot drink. As she waited for the milk to warm she told herself firmly that there was a very good chance that Benedict had simply come home and even now was asleep in his apartment. She hadn't heard him come home but, then, she wouldn't because his apartment faced the outside of the complex while hers faced the courtyard in the centre.

Taking the drink back to bed with her, she sipped it while going over the events of the evening in her mind. She'd been surprised to find Benedict and Andrea together, but when she really thought about it there was no reason why they shouldn't have been. She'd known that Andrea had fancied Benedict from the moment he'd arrived on the unit. And now it looked as if she was just going to have to get used to seeing them together. The force of her emotion had shocked her when she'd seen the pair of them dancing together. After all, what right did she have, feeling such jealousy? Benedict wasn't hers, and Andrea was her friend. She should be happy for them.

But how could she be happy when she was feeling so miserable? What was it Samir had said? Something about being true to yourself. But what exactly did that mean? Samir quite obviously had guessed how she was feeling about Benedict because, if what Cheryl had said was true, he, too, was feeling the same way about Andrea. That had been a surprise, she had to admit. She'd had no idea the Romanian doctor felt that way about her friend. So, surely, what he'd been implying had been that she shouldn't deny her feelings. But how could she let Benedict, or anyone else for that matter, know how she was feeling when she had Miles to consider?

On the other hand, if her feelings for Miles were true, why was she feeling this way about Benedict? Maybe what she really had to do was to examine her feelings for Miles.

Be true to yourself—was this what Samir had meant? And, if it was, why didn't he practise what he preached and let Andrea know how he felt about her?

Did she love Miles? She'd thought she did. But maybe it wasn't love at all because, if it was, surely she wouldn't be feeling this way about another man. She had to admit that her relationship with Miles had been far from easy, but that had come about, she felt, through no fault of their own. Rather it had arisen from the distance between them and Miles's ongoing commitment to his ailing father. She admired him for that but couldn't deny that it had presented many difficulties.

Round and round through the small hours of the night her thoughts rotated as she sought to find a solution to her dilemma.

She slept at last, without reaching any conclusions, but when she awoke and her brain was empty it became crystal clear what it was she had to do.

Sophie was on a late shift that day, which meant going into work at midday. It also meant being fully involved with the children's Christmas party, which was to be held in the paediatric unit at four o'clock.

When she arrived on the ward she found William recovering well from his tonsillectomy. 'I told you, didn't I,' she said, 'that you'd soon feel much better?'

William nodded and grinned. 'Me and Tom have been playing board games. Antonia played some with us but then she was too tired to play any more and Sister said she had to rest.'

Sophie glanced across to Antonia's corner where the curtains were partly drawn around her bed. She'd already heard during report on starting her shift that Antonia's strength was deteriorating.

'She's ill, isn't she?' said William, his round face serious.

Sophie nodded. 'Yes,' she said quietly, 'she is. Very ill.'

'I wish we could help her,' said William.

'You do,' said Sophie with a smile, 'just by being her friend.'

'Will she be able to come to the party?' asked Tom, joining in the conversation for the first time.

'Well, if she rests now she may be able to,' Sophie replied.

'Nathan's been making a lot of noise,' said Tom. 'He didn't want to have a bath.' He paused. 'Will he come to the party?'

'Of course he will,' Sophie replied. 'He'll enjoy a party.'

'Will he?' said William doubtfully. 'I never know when he's enjoying something or when he's hating it.'

Sophie moved on, leaving the two boys playing Snakes and Ladders. Another child had been admitted to the ward that morning, a seven-year-old girl called Kirsty Maitland who'd been involved in a road traffic accident. She'd been taken by ambulance to the accident and emergency unit of St Winifred's, where X-rays had been taken and her injuries assessed. She'd been found to have a fractured left femur, severe lacerations to her face and down the left side of her body, a fractured radius in her left arm, head injuries and a ruptured spleen.

On arrival on Paediatrics after a visit to Theatre it had been decided to place her in one of the side wards in view of the severity of her injuries. When Sophie reached the ward and went in, she found the child's mother by her bedside.

The woman, red-eyed and distraught with weeping, looked up at Sophie as she approached the bed. 'I still can't believe it's happened,' she said. 'I told her time after time to look both ways when she crossed the road... My neighbour told me that the car appeared from nowhere. It was one of those with the blacked-up windows and the thumping music—you know what I mean?'

Sophie nodded. 'Yes,' she replied, 'I do, only too well.'

'She said it was speeding—much too fast for a built-up area. Kirsty was halfway across the road.'

'Then she may well have looked before she stepped off the kerb,' said Sophie.

'She didn't stand a chance.' The woman began sobbing again.

'Come on, Mrs Maitland, upsetting yourself won't help Kirsty or you,' said Sophie gently. She placed her hand on the woman's shoulder then turned to look at the child on the bed. She was sedated and looked very pale beneath the swathe of bandages around her head. Her left leg, which had been plastered, was suspended in a cradle while her left arm was resting on the white cellular blanket that covered the rest of her. A drip had been set up on her right side and Sophie checked this, before checking the little girl's pulse.

'Do you think she'd like a drink of water?' Mrs Maitland leaned forward anxiously.

'Not yet,' Sophie replied. 'But what I am going to do is moisten her lips with a cotton bud, then we'll freshen her up a little. You can help me if you like.'

By the time Sophie had finished making Kirsty more comfortable and had returned to the main ward, it was to find that preparations for the children's party were well under way. Jefferson had brought up trays of goodies prepared by the kitchen staff, Christmas music was playing at one end of the ward and those children who were well enough to join in were grouped around two of the play tables that had been pushed together and covered with a brightly coloured cloth decorated with Disney characters.

Antonia's family was all there and Tom's father and his grandmother had just arrived. Nathan's parents and his sister were grouped around his bed and Sophie was pleased to see that even William's mother had made the effort to be there.

Sophie was carrying a pile of crackers and party poppers to the table when she caught sight of Benedict. He had just come onto the ward and had stopped to talk to Antonia and her family. It was the first time she'd seen him since the previous evening and her heart gave that old familiar lurch that it always did these days when she caught sight of him. Andrea was off duty that day so at least Sophie didn't have to see them together and speculate even further on what might have happened the night before.

A few moments later Benedict left the Brett family and came and stood beside Sophie as she set out the crackers and poppers. He watched her for a while then said, 'Are you all right, Sophie?'

'Of course,' she replied almost flippantly. 'Why wouldn't I be?'

'No reason.' He shrugged. 'I just thought you looked a bit strained, that's all.'

'Too many parties, I expect.' She spoke in the same light tone but inside she was screaming. Of course I look strained! Who wouldn't? I was awake all night, imagining all sorts of terrible things, and I'm now on the verge of ending a relationship with a man I thought I was in love with... And it's all your fault! Instead, calmly she heard herself say, 'Is Father Christmas on his way?'

'He is.' Benedict chuckled, that rich, warm chuckle, the sound of which threatened to turn her bones to water. 'The last I saw of him he was securing his whiskers.' He paused and looked around. 'How's the little Maitland girl?'

'She's comfortable.' Sophie nodded.

'She was in a bit of a mess when they brought her into Theatre.'

'Any permanent damage?'

'It's a bit uncertain. Franklin wants her to have another scan then let the neuro boys have a look at her. That was a nasty bash she had there—especially to her head.'

'Have they got those responsible?'

'Apparently, yes—a carload of young tearaways, from what I hear.'

'I guess she's lucky to be alive.' Sophie paused as she became aware that Benedict was watching her closely. In a desperate effort to avert his attention away from herself, she said, 'What time is Father Christmas arriving?'

'About four forty-five, I believe. I understand the children should have finished eating by then. Did you know that he's also hired a puppet show for afterwards?'

'I heard a whisper. He's a kind man.'

'He loves the kids, there's no doubt about that. Sophie…?' he suddenly touched her arm and she jumped as if she'd been shot.

'I must get on,' she said frantically.

'I'm concerned about you.'

'There's no need…'

'Sophie…' Sister Bailey suddenly appeared. 'Can we set this food out now?'

'Yes, of course.' Sophie nodded and at the same time escaped from Benedict's concerned gaze.

She was busy after that, too busy to talk to Benedict as they laid out the food for the party then supervised the children as they pulled crackers, let off poppers and streamers and ate their food.

The excitement of Father Christmas's visit came next as a heavily disguised Mr Crowley-Smith arrived on the ward. Resplendent in red coat, hat, trousers and shiny black boots, his magnificent white beard and hair curled around his face. From the bulky sack, which he carried on his shoulder, he produced gift-wrapped parcels for each child, including one for Kirsty which was left on the end of her bed for when she woke up, together with a cracker and a heart-shaped balloon which Sophie tied to the bedpost.

By the time the children had enjoyed their puppet show and had all been settled down for bed, Sophie was quite exhausted. 'It was all worth it, though, just to see their faces when Father Christmas arrived and later when they were watching those puppets,' she told one of the night staff as they came on duty.

When she finally reached her apartment, her resolve was every bit as strong as it had been that morning but, having had all day to think about it, she was worried about which method she should choose. While she was absolutely certain that she no longer loved Miles, and that their relationship had to end, she was also very well aware that he might take the news badly and that her timing could be very unfortunate. Christmas wasn't the best time of the year to impart bad news, and it could simply be adding to Miles's troubles if, as he'd said, his father had indeed had a relapse.

Maybe she should wait until after Christmas, but even then how should she do it? A telephone call seemed rather brutal, so maybe it should be in a letter or, failing that, perhaps she should even consider a trip to his home to tell him face to face. The very thought of that filled her with foreboding but maybe that was the only decent thing to do in the circumstances.

She was very well aware that there might now be no chance with Benedict if, as it seemed, he'd begun a relationship with Andrea, but the one thing it had shown her was that she certainly wasn't in love with Miles. What she felt for Benedict, brief as it had been, she'd never before felt for anyone else, including Miles.

She was still wrestling with the problem when her doorbell sounded. She wasn't sure who she was expecting—her parents perhaps, or even Andrea—so when she found Benedict on her doorstep her surprise was total.

'May I come in?' he asked. His manner seemed strange, not evasive exactly but unusual and not like him at all, and when she hesitated he said, 'Please, Sophie, I need to talk to you.'

She stood aside and he walked past her. As he prowled around her sitting-room she sensed a sort of tension about him, almost as if he were the bearer of bad tidings.

'Benedict...' she stood in the doorway, watching him. 'Is there anything wrong?'

He had his back to her, supposedly studying one of the porcelain figurines that had belonged to her grandmother, but he turned at the sound of her voice and stared at her. He still looked tired, his hair was more tousled than usual and there was deep shadow on his jaw. He was wearing a black sweatshirt and jeans and his feet were bare inside the loafers he wore. It looked as if he hadn't intended coming out that evening, as if something had suddenly happened to make him do so.

'Yes,' he said. 'I think there is something wrong.'

'What is it?' She came right into the room, pushing the door to behind her. 'Is it something at work? Is it Antonia?' she asked suddenly in alarm.

'No. No, it isn't Antonia. Sit down, Sophie, there's something I have to tell you. I really don't know quite how to go about it, but it has to be said.'

'You're making me very nervous.' She perched uncertainly on the arm of the sofa but Benedict remained standing, facing her now across the room. 'I can't imagine whatever this can be about.'

'What exactly do you know about Miles Fraser?' he said at last.

Sophie had no idea what she'd been expecting but it certainly hadn't been this. 'What on earth do you mean?' She stared at him in astonishment.

'Please.' He ran his hand through his hair. 'This is very difficult, but try and bear with me. What do you know about him?'

'I told you most of what I know.' Sophie shook her head. 'He lives near Manchester and he's a medical rep for Panasonium Laboratories.'

'What about his private life? How much do you know about that?'

'That he lives with his father who's seriously ill with Parkinson's disease...'

'And?'

'What do you mean—and?'

'Well, is that all?'

'More or less, yes.' She shrugged.

'You haven't visited his home?'

'No. The opportunity never arose. I suggested it once but he said it was very difficult with his father there. Apparently he gets very distressed if there's anyone else in the house...so in the end it always seemed simpler for Miles to come down here to see me.'

'Only half the time he didn't.'

'What do you mean?' Sophie looked up sharply.

'Well, it sounded to me as if he kept letting you down at the last minute.'

'That's true, but it was only because of his father. That was the reason he didn't come down this weekend. His father had had a relapse.'

'So how did you leave things with him?'

'He says he has to come south for his firm in the second week in January. He's arranged respite residential care for his father and he suggested we go down to Cornwall for a few days.'

'And how do you feel about that?' Benedict asked quietly.

Sophie stared at him, her heart thumping wildly. What should she say? For a moment she was on the defensive, wanting to ask him what concern it was of his what she did, then she floundered, uncertain what to say, and she slumped slightly. What did it matter now?

But before she could say anything Benedict spoke again. 'Did he never talk about other relationships, previous partners—that sort of thing?'

She shook her head. 'No, not really. There have been others, there must have been. I'm not that naïve. He's an attractive man but— Benedict, just what is this? What's it all about?'

'There's no easy way of telling you this, Sophie, but I've been talking to Franklin.'

'Franklin? Mr Crowley-Smith?'

'It was all to do with the staff party,' said Benedict with a nod. 'You see, Franklin had previously asked me who I was taking to the party and I'd told him I hoped that you would be coming with me. Anyway, after you'd told me about you and Miles I guess I must have been a bit down at work and Franklin noticed. He asked me what was wrong and I told him that you had someone else.

'As I was telling him I remembered that you'd said Miles Fraser knew Franklin, so I just happened to mention who it was who you were seeing. Franklin seemed surprised but he didn't say anything at that time. He did, however, have more to say today.'

'What do you mean?' Sophie stared at him.

'Franklin is a great one for checking his facts and it seems he did a little checking on Miles Fraser. I'm sorry, Sophie—like I say, there's no easy way of saying this—but I'm afraid Miles is married.'

In the silence that followed, the only sounds were outside—the distant hum of the traffic and the far-off wail of a police siren.

'Married?' Sophie exclaimed incredulously at last. 'Of course he isn't married!'

'Franklin says he remembers Miles from when he was working at Manchester General. Apparently Miles used to visit all the hospitals on the northern circuit on behalf of Panasonium Laboratories and he was very well known amongst the staff. The one thing Franklin particularly remembers is going into the hospital social club one evening several years ago and finding a party in full swing. It turned out to be a party to celebrate Miles Fraser's wedding. I'm sorry, Sophie, I know this must be a shock...'

She continued to stare at him but now it was in disbelief instead of surprise.

At last, from somewhere, she found her voice. 'He can't be married... He can't be,' she said, shaking her head. 'I would have known. I'm sure I would... Maybe he's divorced now or separated or something and he just never told me...'

'He has two children, Sophie,' said Benedict gently.

'What?' She stared at him, aghast.

'Franklin checked him out,' said Benedict. 'I was worried about you. It appears he's notorious as a womaniser at the various towns he visits. Even I thought I'd heard his name somewhere when you first mentioned it but I couldn't quite remember where or in what context... I guess I must have heard some gossip about him at my previous hospital.'

'But what about his father?' said Sophie wildly. 'He lives with his father, for heaven's sake. His father's so ill, he has Parkinson's.'

'No, Sophie.' Benedict crossed the room, then took her hands as he stood before her. 'There *is* no elderly father. Miles Fraser lives in a suburb of Manchester with his wife and children.'

Afterwards, when Sophie looked back on that evening, she wasn't sure what had been the greater shock—finding out that Miles was married, that he had children, or that the father whom he'd used so often as an excuse quite simply didn't exist. Later there was to be anger that she'd been so deceived, but at the time she was only aware of the shock.

Benedict took charge after that, drawing her to her feet and into his arms where he simply held her close for a long while. Then he left her, disappearing briefly—presumably to his own apartment—only to return with a bottle of brandy. He poured equal measures into two of Sophie's glasses then joined her where she was sitting on the sofa in a sort of numb haze and handed her a glass.

'Come on,' he said when she stared blankly at him, 'drink this. You'll feel better. You've had a shock—it'll do you good.'

Suddenly she felt cold, very, very cold, and she began to shiver, her teeth chattering against the glass as she attempted to take a sip. With an exclamation of concern Benedict leaned over and turned up the gas fire.

Gradually warmth crept into her—from the fire, and from the brandy as it seemed to flow into her very veins. Benedict, sitting close beside her on the sofa, slipped an arm around her shoulders and for a long time they sat in silence, staring into the fire.

It was Benedict who eventually broke the silence. 'Did you love him very much?' he asked softly.

'What?' Sophie turned her head, as if she were coming out of a trance, and stared at him.

'Miles Fraser,' he said.

'What about him?' Sophie looked blank.

'I asked if you loved him.'

'I thought I did…once,' she said, and there was no mistaking the bitterness in her voice.

'You'll get over it,' Benedict said gently. 'It must be terrible to know he's deceived you so much, but the hurt will get better—I promise you.'

How gullible she'd been! How stupid! She should have known when he'd made all those excuses. She should have guessed. But she hadn't, not for one minute had she even suspected. She'd believed him, believed all those stories about his poor old father who was so desperately ill. She'd even admired him, for God's sake, for caring for his father when so many would have simply abandoned a frail, utterly dependent old man.

Gradually, as the shock receded it was replaced by another emotion, this time a steadily growing anger.

'Benedict.' She half turned, at the same time drawing away from him. 'Would you mind leaving now?' she said quietly.

'Will you be all right?' he asked doubtfully.

'Perfectly all right.' Her voice was controlled now. 'There's something I have to do.'

CHAPTER TWELVE

BENEDICT had still been worried about Sophie but in the end she'd told him she would be perfectly all right. She was still angry but by the time she dialled the number of Miles's mobile phone an icy calm had begun to creep over her.

He answered almost immediately.

'Miles?'

'Sophie?' He sounded amazed.

'Yes.'

'It didn't sound like you.' He paused. 'Why are you phoning?'

'Inconvenient, is it, Miles?'

'Er…yes, it is a bit…'

'Seeing to your father?'

'Yes… I've left him sitting on the side of the bed—I may have to dash in a moment. But I was going to phone you tomorrow—you know, Christmas Eve and all that.'

'Yes, Miles, I know that was the arrangement, but I couldn't wait that long. I had to speak to you tonight.'

'Ah.' His voice softened. 'Well, that's nice. I'm glad to hear that you're missing me. How did your party go?'

'It went very well. Pity you missed it.'

'Yes, it was. But there you are, these things can't be helped. Now, look, my love.' He lowered his voice. 'I really will have to go but, like I say, I shall phone you tomorrow.'

'What time do you intend phoning?'

'I thought some time during the evening—will that be all right?'

'Won't you be busy then?'

'You mean with Dad? Well, I dare say I could get him settled down early…'

'No, I didn't mean with your father, Miles, I meant with it being Christmas Eve.'

'Sorry?'

'Well, isn't there something you have to do on Christmas Eve?'

'I'm not with you, Sophie.'

'I thought you might have stockings to fill.'

'Stockings…?'

'Isn't that what all fathers do on Christmas Eve?'

There was a long silence on the other end of the phone then very carefully he spoke again. 'I'm sorry, Sophie, I haven't the faintest idea what you're talking about.'

'Oh, yes,' she replied. 'Yes, Miles, I think you have. And if you aren't filling stockings I would imagine there will be a hundred and one other jobs to do to help your wife.'

There was another silence then, taking a deep breath, she said, 'You took me for a fool, Miles, didn't you? A silly, naïve, gullible fool, and I fell for your lies as I don't doubt others have done before me.'

'Now, hang on a minute, Sophie… I don't know who you've been talking to—'

'As it happens, a very reliable source, and I won't hang on. I think you're despicable, Miles, and I feel desperately sorry for your wife and children. But more than that I pity you for being such a sad, pathetic individual that you had to invent a sick old man as an alibi.'

'Sophie, please, calm down.'

'How dare you tell me to calm down?' she said. 'Besides, I'm perfectly calm.'

'Someone has obviously been spreading malicious rumours about me and you're overwrought because of what you've heard...'

'No, Miles, I don't think what I've heard is either rumour or malicious. I actually believe what I've been told is the truth.'

'So you're choosing to believe someone else rather than me?' He was starting to sound angry now. 'You're putting our relationship into jeopardy over this...this gossip!'

'No, Miles,' Sophie said evenly, 'I'm not putting our relationship into jeopardy. I'm ending it—and not because of this, as it happens. The fact is, I'd already made up my mind to end it before I heard about this.'

'I don't understand... Why?'

'For the simple reason that I realised I didn't love you. I've had my doubts that the relationship wasn't going anywhere for a long time now and it looks as if my intuition has proved me right. I don't want to hear from you again, Miles.'

'But, Sophie, come on, be reasonable.' His voice took on a pleading note. 'Just think of all the good times we've had.'

'No, Miles. It's over.'

'I'll come down—as soon as Christmas is over, I'll come down. None of this needs to make any difference to us. Things haven't been good between my wife and I for a long time. You have to believe me, Sophie. What we have, you and I, is something special. One more night together and you'll have no further doubts, I promise you...'

Sophie could feel her anger, which she had until that moment kept under rigid control, begin to rise again. 'Miles,' she said tightly, 'I mean what I'm saying, and if you ever try to contact me again I shall phone your superior at Panasonium Laboratories and tell him how you fiddle your expense account to cover your illicit liaisons. And if that doesn't stop you, I shall write to your wife.'

'You wouldn't... You...' he began to splutter.

'Just watch me.' With a loud click she replaced the receiver.

She felt better in the immediate aftermath, and it was only later that she had to battle with yet more anger and pain—the anger that came from humiliation and the pain that had come from being betrayed and deceived.

So much made sense now—the fact that he hadn't wanted her to go to his home, the fact that he'd only given her a mobile phone number to contact him, and the many times he'd had to change their plans at the last moment. She'd never suspected he was married. If she had, she would never have embarked on a relationship that would inevitably lead to heartbreak. His stories of his father had seemed so plausible and so full of compassion and pathos that she'd never doubted their authenticity.

It was much later that the relief began to creep in—a mere trickle at first, then, as the full realization hit her, almost a tidal wave. It was all over, and in the end that which she'd so feared, namely hurting Miles by telling him that their relationship was over, hadn't come into it.

She was free now, free to do what she wanted. As the thought hit her that where Benedict was concerned she might be too late,

a fresh pain twisted, knife-like, somewhere under her ribs.

While she'd been supposedly otherwise engaged with Miles, Andrea had entered the
arena and staked a claim on Benedict's affec-
tions. Andrea was her friend—how could she
now betray her? And what of Benedict himself? He'd certainly shown a great interest in
her, Sophie, but when he'd found out about her
relationship with Miles he'd seemed to have
transferred that interest to Andrea, if what
she'd seen at the staff party was anything to
go by. The idea of what had happened after
the party had grown in her mind out of all
proportion, even though she knew in her heart
of hearts it was only supposition.

But whatever it was, she told herself in des-
peration, surely now it was all too late?

There was an air of anticipation and suppressed excitement on the ward the following
day, with at least two of the children waiting
with bated breath to see if they would be allowed to go home for Christmas Day.

'When will Mr Crowley-Smith come and see me?' demanded Antonia for the hundredth time.

'It's nearly time for the doctors' round,' said Sophie as she carefully counted out the little girl's medication from the drugs trolley.

'He will let me go, won't he?' Antonia demanded anxiously as she took the tablets and began swallowing them with the help of a tumblerful of water.

'We hope so,' Sophie replied carefully. She didn't want to commit herself too much just in case the paediatrician didn't feel that Antonia was strong enough to make the journey to her home and back again to the ward all in one day.

'I'll promise to be good,' said Antonia. 'I'll rest before I go and come straight to bed when I get back...'

'And what about while you're at home?'

'Mummy has made a bed for me on the sofa and Daddy said he'd draw the sofa right up to the dining-room table so that I can join in the Christmas dinner with everyone. My grandma and grandad will be there as well... And then, after dinner we'll have presents round the tree... They said they'd save the presents till then—even Fleur said she'd wait. I've never known her to wait to open her presents before—usually she rips all the paper off at about five o'clock in the morning.'

'Well, it'll be a very special occasion if you are able to join them,' said Sophie. As she turned back to the drugs trolley she found that there was a lump in her throat as she remembered that the reason the occasion was so special was that it would be Antonia's last Christmas.

A little later, after she'd finished the medication run and was in the treatment room, returning the drugs and setting up a trolley with dressings for Kirsty, she was joined by Andrea. She was still a bit apprehensive where her friend was concerned, knowing Andrea to be smitten with Benedict and more than ready to embark on a full-scale romance with him.

'Have you got over Miles not coming down?' Andrea asked casually as she began sorting through some supplies.

Sophie nodded. 'Yes, I have, as it happens,' she replied. Then after a slight pause, she added, 'Actually, I've ended the relationship.'

Andrea looked up sharply. 'Why did you do that?'

'Because I came to the conclusion that I didn't love him. I'd felt for a long time that the relationship wasn't going anywhere and then, after I'd made up my mind to end it, I found out that Miles had lied to me.'

'Lied to you?'

'Yes, Andrea. You see, the fact is, he's married—'

'What?' Andrea stared at her. 'And you had no idea?'

Sophie shook her head. 'No. I think I must have been incredibly stupid or something but, no, I didn't suspect. He was very plausible and I actually believed his stories about his sick father.'

'You mean, all that wasn't true?' Andrea looked astonished.

'That's right. It just provided a very useful alibi when he couldn't get away. He also has two children.'

'Oh, Sophie, I'm so sorry...' said Andrea. She looked genuinely shaken.

'It's all right.' Sophie shrugged. 'Thank God I found out before I made an even bigger fool of myself. I'd even thought I would go up to Manchester to see him after Christmas rather than end things over the phone. Just imagine me knocking at his door and being confronted by his wife.' Sophie shuddered, as she always did whenever she imagined that particular scenario.

'But…but how did you find out?' There was a puzzled expression on Andrea's face now. 'About him being married, I mean.'

'Oh.' Sophie hesitated for a moment but there was no point in trying to hide the truth. 'Benedict told me,' she said at last.

'Benedict?' Andrea stared at her.

'Yes.' Sophie took a deep breath. 'Look, Andrea, I know you and he have got something going, and you needn't worry—he was only acting purely as a friend towards me. Apparently, he was talking to old Franklin who, believe it or not, actually happened to know Miles in the old days when he was working at Manchester General. Anyway, he told Benedict that he remembered Miles getting married and that as far as he knew he also had children. It seems he also had a reputation for collecting gullible women on his travels. All

Benedict was doing was warning me...
Honestly, Andrea...'

'Really?' Andrea raised one eyebrow.

'Yes. Listen, like I said, I know you and
Benedict—'

'No, Sophie, you know nothing,' said
Andrea with a sigh. 'There's nothing between
Benedict and me.'

'But I thought... You know, the staff party
and everything... I thought...'

'Yes, well.' Andrea shrugged. 'I don't deny
I would have liked there to have been something. As you know, I fancied him something
rotten when he first came here, but I soon
found out I was flogging a dead horse where
he was concerned.'

'Whatever do you mean?' Sophie stared at
her friend.

'Well, take the night of the party, for ex-
ample.'

'Go on.' Sophie frowned.

'Do you know what he did for the entire
evening, not only at the club but afterwards
when he took me home and all the while we
were drinking the coffee I made him?'

'No,' said Sophie faintly, wondering what on earth she was about to hear.

'He talked about you,' said Andrea flatly.

'Me?'

'Yes. Constantly. And even when I brought the conversation round to something else, he very cleverly twisted it back to you again. And now, after hearing what you've just said, I don't for one moment imagine his conversation with old Franklin was just a chance one. No,' she went on, not giving Sophie a chance to comment, 'I would say he sought him out to get the low-down on this Miles character.'

'Oh, I don't think—' Sophie began.

'Don't you?' said Andrea. 'I do.' She paused. 'I bet you'd told Benedict that Miles and Franklin knew each other, hadn't you?'

'Well, yes, I had mentioned it, as a matter of fact.'

'Well, there you are, then. Anyone could see the other night when you came into the club and said that Miles couldn't get down yet again because of his father that something fishy was going on. And Benedict, feeling the way he did about you, certainly wasn't going to swallow it.'

'Oh,' said Sophie.

'So there you are,' said Andrea with a little shrug. 'He's all yours. I'd snap him up quickly, if I were you, before someone else stakes a claim on him.'

'Oh, Andrea.' Sophie stared at her friend. 'I don't know what to say.'

'Don't say anything. Just do it.'

'But what about you?'

'What about me? I dare say there'll be someone else coming along in time.'

'Actually, Andrea,' Sophie said, then paused.

'Yes?' said Andrea.

'There's something I think I should tell *you*.'

'And what's that?'

'Well, at the party the other night I had a long chat with Samir...'

When the doctors arrived on the ward for their morning round there was no sign of the consultant paediatrician.

'You'll have to make do with me this morning,' said Benedict in answer to Sister's question. 'Mr Crowley-Smith is in a meeting.'

'Very well,' said Sister Bailey. 'Sophie, will you accompany us, please?'

As they moved down the ward Benedict hung back fractionally. 'Are you all right?' he murmured to Sophie out of the side of his mouth.

'Yes, I'm fine, thanks,' she whispered back.

'Did you speak to him?'

She nodded.

'I dare say he got one hell of a shock.' Benedict's jaw tightened.

'I'll tell you about it later.'

'Lunchtime in the canteen?'

She nodded again then was forced to concentrate as they'd reached Antonia's bed and Sister was turning to consult Benedict.

'Did Mr Crowley-Smith leave any instructions regarding Antonia?' she asked.

'He's leaving things to my discretion,' Benedict replied briefly. Moving forward, he leaned over the rail at the foot of the bed. 'Good morning, Antonia. How are you this morning?'

'I'm ever so well,' said Antonia, struggling to sit up. Glancing anxiously from one to the other of the group around her bed, she said, 'Isn't Mr Crowley-Smith here this morning?'

'No, Antonia, he isn't—' Sister Bailey began.

'Oh, no…' Antonia wailed, and her eyes began to fill with tears.

'It's all right,' Benedict hastened to reassure her, moving round the bed. Ignoring Sister's glare, he sat on the side. 'Mr Crowley-Smith said I could decide about you going home tomorrow.'

'Oh,' said Antonia.

'Are you sleeping well?' asked Benedict.

'Oh, yes,' said Antonia. 'And I'm eating, aren't I, Sophie?'

When Sophie nodded, Benedict went on, 'And what about your pain?'

'It's OK after I've had my injections and my tablets. Oh, please, Dr Ben, please, may I go home? I promise I'll rest, and I'll come back exactly when you say I have to. I promise… Oh, please…'

'How can I refuse?' said Benedict with a smile.

As Sophie breathed a sigh of relief she glanced round and saw amongst those gathered around the little girl's bed several moist pairs of eyes.

They moved on to Tom after that and, after studying his care plan and medication chart, it was decided that he, too, could go home for Christmas Day and possibly Boxing Day.

'Will his father be in today?' asked Benedict as they moved away from the corner where Tom was playing.

'He usually comes in about mid-afternoon,' replied Sophie.

'In that case, I'll come back,' Benedict replied. 'I want to put it to him that they visit Tom's mother together.'

'Won't you have gone off duty by then?' asked Sister Bailey.

Benedict shook his head. 'No, I intend staying around for the carol-singing at teatime. Now, is there anyone else who can go home?' He looked around the ward. 'Kirsty obviously has to stay. What about Nathan?'

'It's been decided that he stays,' Sister replied. 'He doesn't really know any difference and I think it'll be less stressful for his family at the moment if they come here to see him tomorrow.'

'And William?' Benedict raised his eyebrows.

'Well his tests have been completed and medically he could be discharged...'

'He wants to stay,' said Sophie softly.

'Would that be a problem?' asked Benedict, glancing at Sister Bailey.

She shook her head. 'Apart from emergencies, there won't be any further admissions until the end of the week. I think William will be better off with us over the Christmas period.'

They moved on, assessing the other children on the ward as they went, but all the while Sophie was aware of a steadily growing sense of excitement as it gradually sank in that not only was she now free to pursue a new relationship but that Benedict also was free and not in any way involved with Andrea.

Benedict was already there, waiting for her, when she reached the staff canteen. Sitting in a window-seat, he was scanning a newspaper and was unaware of her approach until she was standing almost directly in front of him. He looked up and as his eyes met hers his expression softened.

'Come and sit down,' he said, rising to his feet and pulling out a chair for her. 'I haven't ordered anything yet. I was going to have toasted teacakes and a pot of tea. Will you join me?'

'I'd love to.' Sophie nodded and sat down. Suddenly she felt weary, as if all the stress and tension of the last few days had caught up with her. For a moment she was content simply to sit and watch as Benedict took charge, ordering their food from the counter and returning a little later with a loaded tray. After he'd sat down again he proceeded to set out the cups, saucers and plates and to pass the teacakes to her.

It wasn't until Sophie bit into a hot teacake, dripping with butter, that she realised she was hungry, and for a while they both remained silent as they ate. It was only then, while Benedict was pouring the tea, that he threw her an anxious sideways glance.

'I've been worried about you,' he said quietly.

'Oh?' she said. Her weariness and hunger satisfied, she was now aware of a glow of contentment that seemed to be stealing over her and cocooning her in its protective warmth.

'Yes.' He nodded. 'It occurred to me last night, after I'd left you, that I may have been utterly insensitive.'

'I don't understand.' She took the cup and saucer he passed across the table to her.

'Well, I was so incensed at that rat's behaviour towards you that I didn't stop to think what your reaction might be. I simply charged in there and told you news which you must have found absolutely devastating, and then I left you to sort things out. I'm so sorry, Sophie, I really am…'

'It's all right, Benedict,' she said gently.

'No.' He shook his head. 'It isn't all right. It must have been a terrible blow to you to find out he was married.'

'Actually,' she said, taking a deep breath, 'it wasn't so much of a blow as you might imagine.

'In fact,' she went on when he stared at her in amazement, 'it did me a bit of a favour so you mustn't blame yourself.'

'I don't understand.' He frowned in bewilderment.

Sophie took a deep breath. 'I was shocked,' she said, 'by what you told me because I really had no idea. I felt humiliated and stupid for not having realised what was going on. But the truth is, I'd already decided to end my relationship with Miles before you told me he was married. What I hadn't been able to decide had been how I should do it.' She swallowed.

Benedict had suddenly grown very still as he listened to what she was saying.

'After the initial shock,' she went on after a moment, 'hearing what you had to say made me very angry and gave me the impetus to make that final phone call. Until you told me, I'd even considered going up to Manchester to see him and tell him face to face that the relationship was over. How glad I am now that I didn't, that you warned me in time what he was really like.'

'But you must be upset because the relationship is over...'

'Not as upset as you might think,' said Sophie slowly. 'You see, I'd had a slightly uneasy feeling for some time that the relationship wasn't really going anywhere—which, of course, it wasn't—but I'd been prepared to give him the benefit of the doubt because of his, as I thought, devoted commitment to his father.'

'So what made you decide to end it?' Reaching out across the table, Benedict covered her hand with his own.

His hand felt warm, and her own safe within it. 'Do you really want to know?' she said, suddenly unable to meet his gaze. 'It's not something I'm particularly proud of.'

'Tell me.' He squeezed her hand as he spoke and she felt a thrill shoot through her.

'It was because of jealousy,' she replied.

'Jealousy?' He raised his eyebrows questioningly and those greenish flecks in his eyes seemed more pronounced than ever.

She nodded. 'It was when I saw you with Andrea in your arms at the staff party. I couldn't bear it, and I knew then that I'd never, ever felt that way about Miles. I didn't love him and I never had.'

His expression as he gazed at her was rapidly becoming one of wonder. 'But there's nothing between Andrea and me—and there never has been,' he said.

'I know that now,' said Sophie ruefully. 'But I didn't know it then, and it hurt... It hurt terribly. But then I worried about Andrea. She's my friend after all, and I knew that she'd been keen on you ever since you came onto the unit.'

'Go on.' There was amusement in his eyes now and he leaned back in his chair, as if suddenly he was enjoying these revelations.

'I told Andrea that I'd finished with Miles and that he was married, and she implied that you'd be pleased. I asked her what she meant and she said that she knew you'd never been interested in her...and...'

'Go on,' he said again, relentlessly.

'And that all the while she'd been with you, you only talked about me.'

There, she'd said it. For one moment she wondered what his reaction would be, but she needn't have worried because as he leaned forward again the tenderest of smiles crossed his features.

'You know something?' he said softly. 'She was absolutely right. I did talk about you. I

talked about you all the time, just as I think
about you all the time. Every waking moment
I think about you, and when I'm asleep I
dream about you.'

As Sophie gazed into his eyes a warmth was
stealing through her veins as she slowly began
to realize that the Christmas she'd been dreading, because she'd thought it was going to be
cold and bleak, was, in fact, going to be pre-
cisely the opposite.

They waited until it was nearly dark before
Sister Bailey turned the lights out in the ward,
leaving just the Christmas-tree lights burning.
Then, with each member of staff carrying a
lighted candle and singing 'O Little Town of
Bethlehem', they processed in single file from
the nurses' station down the centre of the ward
between the beds of wide-eyed children to
stand in a group around the tree.

They sang all the old traditional favourites
and one or two new ones that the children
seemed to know from school.

Once in the flickering candlelight Sophie
caught Samir's eye and he winked conspira-
torially at her while she smiled happily back

at the Romanian doctor. Then, while they were singing 'Silent Night', Sophie found herself watching the children's faces—Antonia who, surrounded by her loving family, was watching the group with a rapt expression on her face and her thin little hands clasped together, Tom who sat on his father's knee with his head on his shoulder, and finally William who'd joined the group and who had hold of Benedict's hand.

And it seemed that in those few precious moments all the hope and sorrow of these people were for that short time bound up in the unconditional love that is Christmas.

Later, after the staff had filed out again, telling the story of the three kings as they went, Sophie returned briefly to the ward before going off duty. The curtains had been drawn around Antonia's bed and her family had retired to the relatives' room, leaving her to rest, but as Sophie peeped in the little girl saw her.

'Sophie,' she called softly.

'You're supposed to be asleep,' said Sophie, slipping inside the cubicle.

'I'm too excited,' said Antonia.

'You must try and sleep,' said Sophie, 'otherwise you'll be too tired to go home for dinner tomorrow.'

'I know,' said Antonia with a sigh. 'Will you be here in the morning, Sophie?'

'Yes, of course I will,' Sophie replied as she leaned across the bed and smoothed the wispy hair back from Antonia's forehead.

'I've been thinking,' she said, 'about your Christmas present.'

'My Christmas present?' said Sophie with a little frown.

'Yes, the one from your grandmother.'

'Oh, you mean my legacy?'

'Yes, that's right.' Antonia nodded. 'It's made you very happy, hasn't it?'

'Yes, it has because I've been able to buy my new home.'

'But your grandmother has died, hasn't she?'

'Yes, Antonia, she has.' Sophie nodded as she got an inkling of Antonia's chain of thought.

'Do you think about her a lot?'

'Yes, I do,' she replied. 'I think about her every day.'

'And do you still love her?' Antonia asked anxiously.

'Of course I do,' Sophie replied unhesitatingly. 'Just because you don't see someone any more doesn't mean you stop loving them.'

Her reply seemed to satisfy Antonia as she snuggled down in her bed and closed her eyes.

Sophie stood watching her for a long moment before, with a little sigh, she quietly stole away.

'You know something?' said Sophie as she rested her head on Benedict's shoulder. It was much later and they were curled up together on the sofa in her flat.

'What's that?' he murmured, holding her a little tighter.

'You made a certain little girl very happy today when you said she could spend Christmas Day with her family.'

He nodded. 'I know. I only hope I've made the right decision.'

'You think it might be too much for her?'

'Maybe. I don't know.'

'But even if it is you've still made her happy, simply by giving her that to look forward to.'

'Yes. You're right.' He brightened at the thought and tightened his hold on her.

'Oh, Benedict,' she said with a sigh of pure contentment, 'I can hardly believe how this has turned out for us.'

He gave a sudden chuckle and she twisted her head to look into his face. 'What is it?' she said. 'Why are you laughing?'

'I was just thinking I would like to have seen your mother's face this evening when you told her about us.'

'Well, you'll be able to see it tomorrow when we go over for tea... *And* my father's,' she added significantly.

'Now you're making me nervous.'

'Just think how it'll be for me when I have to meet all your brood,' she protested.

'They'll love you,' he said. 'I told you how they're always nagging me to settle down. How about we go up and see them for New Year?'

'I shall feel as if I'm under intense scrutiny to see if I measure up to the type of woman they expected you to choose.'

'I'll be by your side. From now on, I'll *always* be by your side.' Looking down at her, he took her face between his hands and gazed into her eyes. 'I love you, Sophie,' he said softly. 'I think I've loved you from the first moment I saw you, right there on the ward when I was helping Harry build his tower. You spoke, I looked up and there you were. You completely knocked me for six, do you know that?'

'No. But tell me about it. I'd like to hear.'

'I wanted you,' he replied simply. 'I wanted you like I've never wanted anyone else. I couldn't get you out of my mind. I could hardly believe my luck when you moved in here.' He glanced around the room as he spoke.

'So why did you take so long in doing anything about it?' Reaching up, Sophie began stroking her finger around his mouth.

'I was terrified of rushing you,' he admitted. 'There seemed something... I don't know... almost nervous about you—'

'It was guilt, actually,' Sophie interrupted drily. 'The temptation was almost proving too much for me as well…'

'Whatever it was, I was afraid that if I came on too strong too soon you'd run a mile. It nearly killed me. I've never had to take so many cold showers in my life! And then when I finally decided it was safe to make a move you floored me by saying you were already spoken for. I simply couldn't believe it. I certainly hadn't got you down as a tease.'

'Which I wasn't!' Sophie protested. 'By that time my feelings were every bit as strong as yours but I felt I had to fight them. If only I'd known!'

'I nearly died of frustration when you turned up alone at the Christmas party,' he said, 'and wearing that dress as well! I don't know how I stopped myself from grabbing you and running off with you.' He gave a deep sigh at the memory.

'And there was me eaten up by jealousy because I thought you and Andrea… And afterwards all I could do was picture the pair of you and what you might be doing together…

Honestly, Benedict, I nearly died that night. I truly thought I'd lost you for ever...'

'Thank God I questioned old Franklin when I did.'

'Even though by then I'd recognised the fact that I wasn't in love with—'

'Don't.' Benedict caught her hand and began kissing her fingers one by one. 'Don't even say his name. I couldn't bear to hear it again because now the waiting is over and I intend to make you mine for all time. Just so you won't be in any further doubt.' Releasing her, he rose to his feet. Reaching out his hand, he took hers and drew her up beside him.

Desire flared somewhere deep inside her as he led her into the bedroom. As they stood in the darkness before the window he enfolded her in his arms.

In the moment before his lips claimed hers in a kiss that sealed their love for all time the midnight bells of Christmas rang out across the town, pealing forth their ancient message of love and hope.

MEDICAL ROMANCE™

Large Print

Titles for the next six months...

July

THREE LITTLE WORDS	Josie Metcalfe
JUST GOOD FRIENDS	Maggie Kingsley
THE PATIENT LOVER	Sheila Danton
THE LOVING FACTOR	Leah Martyn

August

A MOTHER BY NATURE	Caroline Anderson
HEART'S COMMAND	Meredith Webber
A VERY SPECIAL CHILD	Jennifer Taylor
THE ELUSIVE DOCTOR	Abigail Gordon

September

DOCTOR ON LOAN	Marion Lennox
A NURSE IN CRISIS	Lilian Darcy
MEDIC ON APPROVAL	Laura MacDonald
TOUCHED BY ANGELS	Jennifer Taylor

MILLS & BOON®

Makes any time special™

MEDICAL ROMANCE™

—⩙— *Large Print* —⩙—

October

RESCUING DR RYAN	Caroline Anderson
FOUND: ONE HUSBAND	Meredith Webber
A WIFE FOR DR CUNNINGHAM	Maggie Kingsley
RELUCTANT PARTNERS	Margaret Barker

November

CLAIMED: ONE WIFE	Meredith Webber
A NURSE'S FORGIVENESS	Jessica Matthews
THE ITALIAN DOCTOR	Jennifer Taylor
NURSE IN NEED	Alison Roberts

December

COMING HOME TO DANIEL	Josie Metcalfe
DR MATHIESON'S DAUGHTER	Maggie Kingsley
THE NURSE'S DILEMMA	Gill Sanderson
THE HONOURABLE DOCTOR	Carol Wood

MILLS & BOON®

Makes any time special™